"What **my**

"You had no ~~laying~~ your hands on my woman, and if you've trifled with her honor, well, we both know what a man has to do about a thing like *that*."

Longarm snorted in disgust. "You sure worry a lot about your woman's honor for a man who just beat her half to death, and we'll see if it was only half when that nurse gets here."

The man in the doorway raised the muzzle of his twelve-gauge as Longarm took a step toward him. "Don't try nothing. I'll kill you. I mean it," he warned.

TABOR EVANS

LONGARM

ON THE OVERLAND TRAIL

JOVE BOOKS, NEW YORK

LONGARM ON THE OVERLAND TRAIL

A Jove Book/published by arrangement with
the author

PRINTING HISTORY
Jove edition/August 1987

ISBN: 0-515-09113-8

Jove Books are published by The Berkley Publishing Group,
200 Madison Avenue, New York, New York 10016.
The name "JOVE" and the "J" logo
are trademarks belonging to Jove Publications, Inc.

PRINTED IN THE UNITED STATES OF AMERICA

10 9 8 7 6 5 4 3 2 1

Chapter 1

It was a Friday night, so the saloon was crowded when Longarm dropped by after collecting his pay at the nearby federal building for a shot of red-eye and another look at the mighty handsome barmaid they'd just hired.

He could see neither notion figured to be easy. So he'd about decided to try his luck at the Black Cat or Pronghorn when he saw an elbow's worth of mahogany between a townee and a stockman and wedged his taller frame into the gap to see if he could catch the barmaid's eye without violating the civic ordinance forbidding a serious discharge of firearms within the Denver city limits.

The boys had the pretty little thing as busy as a one-armed paper hanger in a windstorm. She was pumping suds and filling shot glasses faster than the Constitution could possibly require. So Longarm was content just to admire her for the moment. He felt no urgent need for more cheer than the sight of her dashing about inspired. He'd always admired perky little blue-eyed blondes.

1

He was reaching for a smoke when someone jabbed him rudely in the ribs from behind and a gruff, albeit high-pitched, voice told him, "You took my place, you sissy-dressed moose!"

Longarm turned to stare thoughtfully down at a wild and wooly apparition far too short to talk so tough. The baby face glaring up at him from the gloom cast by the brim of a black ten-gallon hat looked too young to vote, let alone drink with full-grown men.

The brace of Colt '74s strapped on over a pair of show-off goat-hair chaps had to be taken more seriously than the chaps and black sateen shirt. Nobody that small could be thinking of fighting with his *fists,* and if the cute little rascal wasn't looking for a fight he was putting on a mighty convincing show.

Longarm smiled and said, "Don't get your bowels in an uproar, pard. I didn't know this space had been claimed by anyone as desperate to drink as you must be."

"You know it now," the cocky little bully snapped. "I told this cowboy bastard to save my place whilst I took a leak. I can see he didn't. But that don't matter. You can move or fill your fist for all I care. I like fighting almost as much as I like to screw, and I'm a fiend for screwing."

Longarm saw the much bigger stockman who'd been called a bastard was already moving away fast. Longarm had thought he looked sober. He sighed. "Hold your fire, pard. Far be it from me to stand between a man and his heart's desire," he said.

Then he stepped away from the bar. The runty ruffian looked triumphant. "I never took you for a hairpin with the grit to stand up to *me*. You know my rep, right?" he asked.

Longarm didn't even want to know who he was. The baby face was not on his list of federal wants. It was up to the Denver police to notify the poor little critter's kin when the inevitable caught up with him.

Things were more sensible down at the far end of the bar. By some oversight there was space enough between the wall and the last customer down the line for Longarm to belly up again. As he did so a voice in his ear said, "That was close."

It was the stockman who'd crawfished away from the troublesome fool just ahead of him. Longarm shrugged. "I don't know how close it was. But I admire *your* common sense, too. Us grown men would never get anything done if we stopped to stomp every little fool in our path."

"Didn't you know who he was?" the stockman asked.

Before Longarm could say he really didn't care, they heard a boastful cry for attention and a now-familiar high-pitched voice commenced to sing:

"Gather close around and I'll tell you a tale
Of Black Jack Slade on the Overland Trail
Some say he's dead, some say he was killed
It's a lie, not a drop of my blood was spilled!"

He let go with a wild war whoop that could have burst the hinges of hell, followed it up with a fusilade of .45 lead into the pressed-tin ceiling, and vacated the premises howling like a wolf or perhaps, in fairness to wolves, a mad dog.

As a dead silence descended Longarm nodded soberly. "You was right. That was close. He must be loco."

"That was Black Jack Slade," the stockman assured Longarm. "He told me, hisself, when he asked me to hold his place. I'm sorry about that. He was gone so long I didn't think he was coming back."

Longarm snorted in disgust and replied, "Now *you're* talking loco, too, no offense. In the first place, the one

3

and original Black Jack Slade ain't been with us since the War. He didn't get killed in the War. Vigilantes strung him up near Virginia City, Montana."

"More than one old boy's lived through a casual hanging, you know."

"I was getting to the second place. Black Jack Slade was before my time out here. But I've seen his tombstone in Salt Lake City, and the dates make him a full-grown man of forty when they buried him. That noisy little fool can't be more'n twenty or so. So how could he be a forty-year-old mad killer who died a good fifteen years ago?"

The stockman shrugged. "Mayhaps they're *both* mad killers. I didn't know that much about the one and original Black Jack Slade. I'd only heard the name in connection with a lot of serious hell-raising up around Julesburg."

The blond barmaid was headed their way with a couple of beer schooners. Longarm managed to catch her eye as she put them down for a couple of gents who'd been there first. She nodded at Longarm but turned away to fill other orders. He sighed. "I can see why that damn fool left. A man could die of thirst in here even if he didn't get shot by kids dressed up in winter chaps in August."

The stockman was still interested in the diminutive desperado, for some reason. He asked, "Wasn't it Julesburg where Black Jack Slade carved so many notches on his gun grips?"

Longarm grimaced, reached for a smoke, and said, "Ned Buntline made that up for his *Wild West Magazine*. The first thing you do after you gun a man is to deny it was you as gunned him. You don't keep a record for the law to use against you. They do say the real Black Jack Slade kept the ear of one man he gunned as a watch fob. But, like I say, it was before my time."

"He must have been mean as hell," the stockman opined.

"Well, sure he was mean as hell," said Longarm, lighting his three-for-a-nickel cheroot. "That's how come they lynched him. He was a mean drunk who tortured men to death. Would *you* want a cuss like that for a neighbor?"

The barmaid at last stopped in front of Longarm, smiled wearily, and asked what she could do for him. He was too polite to ask for more than shots and chasers for him and his thirsty pal. As she spun around to dash off again, the stockman said he took his red-eye neat and Longarm said, "That's all right. I'll nurse both the beers. Lord knows when that poor little gal will ever get time to serve drinks one at a time. You wouldn't know her name, would you?"

The stockman didn't. So it took Longarm the better part of an hour to find out her name was Grace. But he was still sober because of the slow service. The place was just beginning to thin out and she was just starting to spend more time at his end of the bar, batting her eyelashes friendly, when a blue-uniformed copper badge came up beside Longarm. "They said you might be here, Longarm. Sergeant Nolan told me to fetch you if I could find you."

Longarm sighed and said, "You found me. What's up?"

"Two federal agents down. The federal building is closed at this hour and the sarge thinks someone working for Uncle Sam may have something to say about the shooting."

"Nolan thought right. You say a couple of deputy marshals lost a shootout? That's odd. I don't recall Billy Vail mentioning anything about us picking anyone up tonight."

The copper badge shook his head. "It wasn't any of

you boys. Couple of gents from the provost marshal's office. Went to pick up an army deserter at the address he'd given on his enlistment papers and got lucky about the address and unlucky about him. Right now they're spread out on the rug over there. It ain't all that far. Are you coming?"

Longarm shot a wistful glance at the blonde down the bar and said, "Let's go get it over with. As the nearest federal officer still sober enough to function, it looks like it *could* be my case for now."

As they elbowed their way toward the batwing doors, Longarm asked if they'd made any arrests yet. The copper badge told him, "No. The kid they was after threw down on them, right in his front parlor, and drilled 'em both through their hearts like a real pro. Time the roundsman on the beat responded to the sound of gunfire on a normally quiet street, the moody cuss was long gone. He might not get far, though. Witnesses gave us a mighty good description to go on."

As they got outside, the copper badge added, "He's a little runt dressed cow, even if he was a townee boy raised right here in the city. Worse yet, he was last seen running in wooly chaps and a hat big enough for a family of Arapaho to move into."

Longarm looked incredulous. "That can't be right! Do we have a name to go with this pint-sized pistoleer?"

The copper badge nodded. "Sure. His name is Joseph, but he makes everyone call him Jack. Jack Slade. What's so funny?"

Longarm said, "It ain't funny. It's just awful. I figured he had to be crazy, but not *that* crazy!"

Copper badges got to walk more than Longarm had to, so their notion of not far was over a quarter-mile, across Broadway and up the lower slopes of Capitol Hill as far as Lincoln Avenue. Longarm had the house figured before they got to it. There was a considerable crowd out front and Sergeant Nolan was standing on the front porch of the modest but neatly painted two-story frame structure.

As they joined him on the porch, Nolan told Longarm, "We got a statement from the only other person in the house, the killer's older sister. Some neighbor women are comforting her in her sewing room. Poor thing's hysterical."

As he followed Nolan in, Longarm asked, "Did his kin see the killing?" "No," Nolan replied. "She didn't even know he'd deserted, riding his commanding officer's horse with the saddlebags full of stuff the army never issued him. When they showed up to ask if he might possibly be home she went to fetch him from his quarters over the carriage house out back. She didn't find him there. As she was coming back she heard two shots, ran into her parlor where she'd left the army agents, and I'm about to show you what she found."

They stepped into the well kept if cheaply furnished parlor. It was occupied by a handful of other lawmen on their feet and two more stretched side by side on the floor. Both were dressed in civilian riding duds. Longarm saw no need to comment on this. In a peacetime army no soldier off-post was required to wear a uniform, and a man who got gigged for every stain or missing button seldom did. Getting close to deserters was tough enough.

Nolan said, "We've already patted them down for I.D. The older one would be Staff Sergeant Flint. The younger one with the big moustache was Sergeant Hughes."

Longarm didn't answer. He stared soberly down at the dead men, feeling embarrassed for them as he noted how dumb and helpless they looked, staring up through him. They were both wearing gun rigs under their coats. He bent to draw Flint's and sniff it.

Nolan said, "Neither gun's been fired, or drawed, for that matter. As we put it together, they were just standing there like big-ass birds when the kid stepped through that doorway, yonder, and simply blowed them away. He must have had his gun out already, don't you reckon?"

"He had *two*, Longarm said. "He fired both at once. In the time it takes to drill one man and recock a single-action '74 the one left would have surely at least *tried*. And you're right, neither made a move to defend himself. Look at how their boot heels line up so neat. They went down together, dead before they hit the rug."

Nolan nodded. "A slug that size through the heart can blow your lights out sudden indeed. But who says they had to be shot with single-action?" he asked.

Longarm said, "Me. I met a sass who couldn't be anyone but the killer no more than an hour or so ago in the Parthenon saloon. He wore a brace of army-issue '74s, and to think I took him for a drunk kid on the prod!"

He went on to bring the others up to date on the one and original Black Jack Slade. They agreed that was crazy, too.

"The punk's last name *is* Slade," Nolan said. "After that he was full of pure bull. We've been canvassing the neighborhood. The killer turned twenty-two this June and looked younger. He went to Evans Grammar School less than a mile from here, but left in the fifth grade after losing some school time to the scarlet fever. He's described by those who know him, including some as went to school with him, as a sickly, feeble-minded runt who's never been able to hold a job. He was sponging off his kin here until about a year or more ago, when his sister's husband told him it was time he supported himself and threw him out."

"That sounds sensible. Where's the brother-in-law right now?"

"Dead. Died last winter whilst the boy was in the army, trying to hold down the only job he could get,

8

with the depression over. We figure he heard his big sister had become a widow and decided to move back in with her. The army must have figured the same way and, as you see, they'd have been better off calling it good riddance to bad rubbish."

Longarm nodded and said, "Some officers can be sort of possessive about their favorite mounts. But you say the neighbors say he left the premises on his own two feet?"

Nolan looked uncomfortable. "One did. An old lady down near the corner who spends a lot of time leaning out her back window, watching out for apple-stealing kids or whatever. She spotted young Joe Slade in the alley out back earlier this evening. She knew who it was because not even the neighborhood kids who steal her apples dress so silly."

"A neighbor would likely know him on sight, even in an alley," Longarm said. "The question now is whether he left for that saloon before or after the shooting. What time did that old lady say she spotted him all dressed up for a Wild West show?"

Nolan looked pained. "Longarm, you know how hard it is for a witness to recall the exact time they witnessed something when they didn't know it was important. All she knows is that she saw him leaving the neighborhood for parts unknown, any time you want her to swear to, as long as it was after sundown. What damn difference can it make?"

Longarm said, "If he gunned two men and then went to drink and pester folk in a nearby saloon, on foot, dressed wild as well, I fail to see how he could still be running loose."

Nolan started to ask what Longarm meant. Then he said, "Yeah, we do have all our men looking for him and he's said to have few if any friends in town. But what if that wild act he put on for you was a slicker? What if he wanted everyone to remember him all

9

decked out out like Buffalo Bill so's that would be what we all went looking for?"

"That works, if we assume young Slade has just now grown more brains than he's ever shown evidence of having before," Longarm said. "We'd better have a look at his quarters. I, for one, will feel dumb as hell if we find a pair of goat-hair chaps hanging on a bed post. Do we need permission from the lady of the house?"

Nolan said, "No. She's been cooperative as hell for a hysterical young widow woman. Come on, I'll show you the way."

They passed down a dark hallway. Through an open doorway Longarm caught a glimpse of an ashen young brunette being rocked in the arms of an older, meaner-looking gal who glared at him as if she thought he was Attila the Hun. He supposed, from their point of view, he was. Lawmen were never too welcome in the house of a wanted murderer.

They went out the back door and crossed a well-tended garden to the carriage house opening on the back alley. The lower level was a cavernous expanse of brick-paved emptiness. Nolan said, "I already asked. Flora Banes, née Slade, and her man didn't keep live or rolling stock, even when he was alive. This close to the center of town, he walked to work. It didn't pay, next to hiring a rig, on the occasions they went somewhere more important."

"What about that army mount?"

"None of the neighbors recall seeing it. The kid showed up on foot in army blues a month or so back. They thought it sort of funny, later, when he commenced to wander about all dressed up like a cowboy, with no horse to chase cows with."

Nolan lit a match and led the way up to the former hayloft. As he lit a wall lamp, Longarm saw that it had been fitted up as a sort of bedroom. In contrast to the rest of the house, it was a mess. The unmade cot was wedged against the sloping rafters, facing a wall that stood straighter, about ten feet away.

"It looks like they built in more than one room up here," Longarm said.

Nolan said, "I asked the widow woman. Her husband used the room next to this as a workshop. He likely used *all* this space before his wife's kid brother moved in to sponge off them. As it is, this is more space than I'd give *my* brother-in-law if he was a lazy idjet who wouldn't even *try* to get a job."

Longarm found a shabby army uniform and a tweed topcoat hanging in a wardrobe. There were some socks and underwear in the top drawer of the washstand. There was no other furniture. But at least a ton of old magazines, not too neatly stacked, took up six or eight feet of floor space, waist high. Longarm said, "He must have liked to read in bed." He casually picked up a well-thumbed pulp magazine and added, "Oh, look at this."

It was a copy of *Deadwood Dick,* published in London, England. Nolan peered over his shoulder. "I didn't know Deadwood Dick had his own magazine. I knew Buffalo Bill did, but I didn't think Deadwood Dick was that important."

Longarm said, "Deadwood Dick don't exist, even though I keep running into him in saloons. One time, up in Deadwood, I met *two* Deadwood Dicks at once."

"I ain't sure I follows your drift, Longarm. How in thunder could anyone meet a man who ain't real?"

Longarm explained, "Deadwood Dick is the creation of an English writer named Charles Perry. In one of the first books he was an outlaw who got killed off, but then Perry brought him back to life as a lawman."

"In London, England?"

"That's where Perry lives. He lets Deadwood Dick go all over the place. He got to fight cannibals in the Weird Islands one time, but he mostly pesters folk here in the American West, or the American West as it looks to folk in London Town."

"But you said you really met him, *two* of him, in Deadwood, U.S. of A."

Longarm shook his head. "I met a couple of old drunks named Richard who lived in Deadwood and somehow decided Perry was writing about *them*. I see there's one about Calamity Jane, here, and she'd sure like this cover, for I've never seen her this skinny and I've known her since she was working for Madame Moustache."

Nolan took the garishly illustrated penny dreadful, held it to the light, and said, "Naw, that ain't her. Can they make up stories about *real* folk as well, Longarm?"

"I once told Ned Buntline I'd sue his ass if he put *me* in one of his magazines, but some old boys get a kick out of it, I reckon. When and if anyone ever gets around to putting down the true history of the things out here, they're going to have one hell of time figuring out who did what, with what, to whom. I see they got Buffalo Bill avenging Custer in this one. Oh, hell, look at this!"

It was two cent's worth of sheet music with a garish orange and purple cover. The title read, "The Ballad Of Black Jack Slade." When Longarm opened it the first line, sure enough, read:

"Gather close around and I'll tell you a tale."

Nolan sighed. "You can't be serious."

Longarm shrugged. "*I* never said he was Black Jack Slade. *He* did. And damned if I don't think he might have *meant* it. I hope I'm wrong. The real Jack Slade was mean as hell."

Chapter 2

When Longarm finally reported for work the next morning, Henry, the clerk who played the typewriter in the front office, shot him a now-you're-gonna-get-it smirk and told him the boss wanted to see him the moment he ever saw fit to show up.

Longarm sighed fatalistically and ambled back to the inner sanctum of U.S. Marshal William Vail to take his chewing like a man.

Old Billy Vail was shorter, fatter, balder, and usually looked meaner than Longarm. But this morning he looked up calmly from behind his cluttered desk, shot a weary glance at the banjo clock on his oak-paneled wall, and said, "Save your excuses. You staked out the nine-thirty northbound Burlington in the vain hope Slade might be headed for his old haunts along the Overland Trail."

Longarm sat down with a sheepish grin. "It was worth a try. You heard about the shootout, eh?"

"I did. This may come as a surprise to you, but the

13

Denver chief of police and the local federal marshal are supposed to remain on speaking terms. A copy of the police report they were kind enough to give *you* a copy of was waiting for me when I arrived to open this very office at the time the taxpayers of these United States expect us to start working for *them*. You've had your fun. Now I want you to go get a shave and a haircut, you untidy rascal. For, Saturday or not, the federal district court down the hall is holding a special hearing, and they asked me to supply a deputy to ride herd on an Indian agent who ought to be ashamed of himself."

Longarm shook his head and said, "Damn it, Billy, this other case is *personal*. I *had* the little maniac and I let him walk away and gun two fellow federal agents. You got to let me make up for my awful mistake last night."

Vail sighed and replied, not unkindly, "I know how dumb you have to be feeling this morning. But, having gone over the whole affair in my head as well as on paper, I can't say I'd have acted a bit different. You had no way of knowing a taproom troublemaker was anybody serious. Walking away from a pointless argument was the mark of a mature individual. So you not only done right, but now that I've read the coroner's report on them army men, it could've been even wiser than you might have thought at the time."

Longarm grimaced. "Aw, crap. I *had* the wild-eyed pissant, Billy. Both ways. The blonde behind the bar could have took him in a wrestling match, and he was toting single-action '74s. I hate to brag, but you've seen me and my double-action .44-40 in action against worse odds."

"I have. You're good. So were them two army agents. That's doubtless how they wound up dead. I calls it the Billy the Kid phenomenon. A phenomenon is like a mirage, only more dangerous."

Longarm said, "I know what a phenomenon is. What

could Billy the Kid have to do with the case? The last I heard, that other little pest was on the dodge down New Mexico way."

Vail leaned back in his own chair to haul out a nickel cigar as he explained, "That other Kid's managed to kill more than one growed man with a rep because, like you and them two dead army men, they hesitated the fraction of a second it takes to wind up dead. I've just gone over little Joseph Slade's known history, up to where he suddenly turned horse thief and killer. It's pathetic as hell. He was too awkward as well as too sickly to engage in shoolyard sports over at Evans. The teachers had to protect him from the usual classroom bullies. One that had him crying to the teacher regular was a ten-year-old *girl*. Nobody cared when he just stopped coming to school one day because, on top of being a crybaby, he was dumb as hell. He was behind all the other kids in reading, spelled awful, and never learned long division at all. Lord knows why the army ever let him join up. I know it's hard to get men at thirteen dollars a month, but you'd think they'd draw the line *some* damn place."

"He was acting a lot tougher last night," Longarm said.

"I ain't finished. I said I just went over the report. It's about a sickly, not-too-bright, lonely boy who read lots of penny dreadfuls until something snapped in his feeble mind. He ain't never been anywheres near Julesburg, and his family ain't in any way related to the real Black Jack Slade. That was easy for the Denver police to check out with a couple of night-rate wires to the county clerks involved. But somehow the broodsome loner must have adopted his namesake as a hero. As the gent he wished he could be. For if there was one thing the original Jack Slade was not, it was a sickly sissy. The kid no doubt read of the time his hero was hit twice with pistol rounds and blasted thrice with a sawed-off

15

shotgun in the same fight. It's a matter of public record that Slade was left for dead, got back up, and tracked down the man who'd gunned him to return the favor, slow. Slade winged his man, tied him to a post, and tortured him to death with fleshshot rounds from the kneecaps up. Then he cut off his ears and ended the discussion by shoving a gun muzzle down the poor bastard's throat and pulling the trigger. Can you imagine the effect this tale must have had on an impressionable youth who'd never won a fight in his life?"

Longarm said, "I can. I saw the bodies he left on his sister's rug. The army must have taught him to handle a gun pretty good in the short time they was graced with his full attention to such matters, and there's some truth to the old saw about Sam Colt having made all men equal. That's why you got to let me go after the young lunatic, boss. For I do know, now, just how dangerous he really is and, more important, I know him on sight. One had to be there to get the joke, Billy. He looks harmless as a kid dressed up for Halloween and we're likely to wind up with a mess of dead lawmen before he runs into one as morose as me."

Vail shook his head, lit his smoke, and shook out the match before he said, in a tone that sounded final, "It ain't our case. The killing took place under Denver jurisdiction. The victims rode for another federal department. We got enough of a caseload as it is. We don't need to go out *looking* for work, old son."

He could see how Longarm felt about that. So he added in an almost fatherly tone, "Look, I know you feel responsible but it wasn't your fault. The provost marshal sent two good men to do a job and they muffed it. So it was *their* fault."

"I could have taken him, Billy."

"No you couldn't have, not knowing what you knew *then*. I don't hire trigger-happy deputies and had you blown away a kid just for sassing you in a saloon I'd

16

have had to fire you or worse. We're *all* smart as hell *after* we make a sensible mistake. Half the damn women in this world would die old maids if the Lord gave us the power to read minds, and poker would be no fun at all."

"I could have told you that. Meanwhile, that deadly dwarf is still running loose out there with two loaded guns!"

Vail shrugged. "We lives in an imperfect world, old son. Our job is to pick up the pests with Justice Department papers out on 'em. You can only eat an apple a bite at a time. We've neither the manpower nor the time to go after every pain in the ass on earth. So don't be greedy. I got plenty of sinners with plenty of Justice Department arrest warrants on 'em, if you really feel ambitious."

Longarm didn't like it, but he knew when Billy Vail meant it, and that would have been the end of it had not Henry come in just then with a telegram to say, "I just signed for this, sir. It's marked 'urgent' and requests a reply."

Vail frowned. "Well, give it to me, Henry. I can't hardly reply to it before I *read* it, can I?"

Longarm leaned back in the leather guest chair and got out a smoke as Vail took the wire and read it, getting redder-faced by the word. Near the end, he was growling like a junkyard dog, deep in his throat.

When he'd finished Vail balled the yellow paper up in a white-knuckled fist and told Henry how to word his reply. The clerk got even paler. "You can't send words like that by Western Union, Marshal Vail!" he protested.

Vail growled, "Word it your way, then, just as long as you tell 'em to take a flying fuck at a rolling wagon wheel!"

As Henry left, Longarm chuckled and asked Vail who he wanted to see injured so dreadfully.

"War Department," Vail said. "Do you remember

17

that prissy Colonel Walthers we had that trouble with down in the coal-mining country a spell back?"

Longarm lit his cheroot. "Who could ever forget him?" he asked. "You were lucky. You only tangled with him a time or two. I've had even *more* trouble with the pompous idjet and his military police. What's he done now? Anyone can see he's got you sort of upset."

"He just warned us the murder of them two army men was the army's case entire, and it seems he remembers you as well. He just mentioned you by name, warning me he'll take it personal if you stick your big nose—his words—into his case before he can get here from Fort Collins with his own team of investigators."

Longarm asked innocently, "Can the army give orders to this here department, boss?"

Vail grinned wolfishly. "They cannot. I thought we had that settled the last time that asshole argued federal jurisdictions with me."

Longarm, who knew his boss better than the pompous Colonel Walthers must have, was already rising to his feet as Marshal Vail roared, "What are you just sitting there for? Go out and *git* me that murderous midget maniac before the damned old army trips over him!"

By two in the afternoon Longarm's stomach was growling and his feet weren't too happy about all the circles they'd been walking in on the sun-baked streets of Denver. He stopped at a Broadway beanery for some chili con carne and apple pie, washed it down with plenty of black coffee, and found out the handsome waitress was married to the short-order cook in the back.

Feeling better, but no smarter, he consulted the list he'd made before leaving the federal building and decided to check out the scene of the crime again, next. He respected the Denver police and the place had surely been combed over pretty well already. But sometimes things looked a mite different by the light of day.

The whole block looked different as he trudged up the slope with the summer sun agreeing that the suit required for work was a mighty dumb notion. The street was now deserted and it could have used some shade trees as well. He hadn't noticed the night before that the Banes house was freshly painted a sort of baby blush pink with white trim, or that the modest front yard was mowed neat as a green plush carpet. It took a lot of water and work to have even a little lawn like that in Denver after, say, the end of June. He stepped up on the porch and twisted the doorbell. The wan-looking lady of the house opened it to say, "Oh, you were here with those other lawmen last night, weren't you?"

She had washed her face and fixed her hair, and she wore a fresh cotton print that harmonized nice with her dark hair and sad blue eyes. He smiled reassuringly down at her and said, "I am Deputy U.S. Marshal Custis Long, Miss Flora. I know I'm intruding and I confess I don't have a search warrant. If you want to slam your door in my face I won't be able to do a thing about it."

She sighed. "Come in. I don't know what you could be looking for now, but you're welcome to look all you like. Have they caught Joseph yet?"

As he followed her inside and into her front parlor he saw that she had removed the rug. He didn't ask why. "If it's any comfort to you, ma'am, I doubt they'll hang your kid brother once I bring him in, and I mean to bring him in gentle as possible," he told her.

She indicated a seat on her leather davenport. "That's a very gentle way of saying you think my brother is insane, and I don't see how you'll ever take him alive. You saw what he did in this very room last night."

Longarm shook his head. "Not really. It was all over by the time I showed up. I know you say you didn't witness the actual fight, neither. But I'd like to go over what you do remember, if you're up to talking more about it, now."

She said, "I've recovered from the first shock. It hit me a lot worse when my husband died not long ago. As you see, I've gotten rid of the well-meaning friends who were more in my way than any real help, and now I'm trying to tidy up the house a bit."

"I noticed, and I think you're dealing with family troubles smart as well as brave, Miss Flora. I've had more experience in these matters than I ever wanted to, and carrying on as usual is a lot less hurtsome than just brooding about things as can't be helped. I suspect I know just how you must feel right now."

She stared up at him sort of glassy-eyed. "No, you don't. It wasn't *your* brother who went crazy and started to kill people for no reason at all!"

He put a gentle hand on her upper arm to steady her and sit her down. He remained standing. "Easy, now. The boy thought he had a reason. Those gents from the provost marshal came here to arrest him. Can you tell me anything abut them? I mean before, not after."

She shrugged. "There's nothing much to tell. I had no idea Joseph had deserted the army until they told me. He said they let him out early because he was sickly, and that hardly seemed like a fib, knowing him as I did. The older officer did most of the talking. He was very pleasant and understanding when I told them I'd had no idea my brother could be in trouble. I offered them some coffee and cake and went to fetch Joseph as they sat here on this very sofa. The rest you know, and—I Heavens, what's come over me? I seem to have forgotten my manners, and I've a pot on the stove I just brewed."

But as she rose to behave more graciously Longarm told her, "I just ate, and this ain't a social call, Miss Flora. I see no reason to poke about your own quarters, even though I'm sure you've dust-mopped in every

20

corner. But I'd sure like to snoop about your old carriage house some more by daylight, if you don't mind."

She said she didn't mind at all and that she'd been meaning to get to that chore in any case. He followed her out the back as she grabbed a broom on the fly. He'd noticed the night before, that the back yard seemed well tended. As he spied the gay flower borders all about he commented on them and said, "You sure keep your property up nice, ma'am. Did your brother help with all this?"

She sighed and said, "Surely you jest," as she led him back inside the carriage house.

The bottom level didn't look as much like a cave with the daylight streaming through the one window facing the house. There was a faint, very faint smell of oats and horse. He dropped to one knee to run a thoughtful finger along the sand between the paving bricks. She asked what he was looking for and he told her, "It ain't delicate to say. But I see you told the copper badges true about that horse your brother is said to have stolen. It ain't hard to clean up after one horse on short notice. But you can't hardly swab out a stable without water, and it's my considered opinion this paving ain't been wet down in recent memory."

"Thank you. I didn't know I was a suspect as well," she said.

He got to his feet, dusting off his knee with his hat as he told her, "Close kin are allowed a few fibs in cases like these. It's only human. I'm only doing my job when I cover all bets."

"Then search his quarters again, so I can clean up the mess he left behind. He wouldn't let me in there to clean when he was still here."

Longarm nodded and led the way up as she followed, broom in hand, like a pretty little witch. She stood in the doorway as he went over the untidy room again by better light. He didn't find anything new and said so, adding, "I'd like to take some of this reading material along with me, if you don't mind."

"Take it *all*, if you like," she said. "I mean to throw it all out in any case. I've never understood how anyone could spend good money on such trash."

He picked the ballad of Black Jack Slade and a couple of Ned Buntlines to go over later as he told her, "You'd do better if you sold all this paper to the junk man next time he comes along the alley, ma'am. You're right about your brother amassing at least a few dollars' worth of pulp paper, here. It must have cost him a mite more, buying 'em one at a time."

She said, "It did. I don't mind telling you it was a bone of contention between my brother and my late husband. Joseph just couldn't resist those silly silly stories about cowboys and Indians and, since we were supporting him . . ."

"It could have been more expensive if he drank a lot," Longarm observed. "Did he?"

She shook her head. "No. Tom often said he'd have more respect for an idler with more manly bad habits. Joseph didn't do much of anything but mope about up here. Tom said it made him more nervous than if he'd played with matches and teased girls."

Longarm nodded understandingly. "Tom would be your late husband, Thomas Banes of the Denver Dry Goods Company. I know these are hurtful questions, but there was nothing on the police records as to how your man happened to pass away."

She said, "I've grown used to answering that. Tom had heart trouble. He died at work. Joseph couldn't have had anything to do with it, if that's what you mean."

Longarm raised an eyebrow. "It wasn't. I already knew your man threw your brother out and that he was in the army miles from here, at the time. But did they really get along *that* badly?"

She shrugged. "Not really. They tended to avoid one another as much as they could. Tom didn't even use his workshop next door, toward the end. I don't mind saying meals were eaten in grim silence until one night Joseph asked me for more money and Tom just clouded up and rained all over him. There might have been a fight, had poor Joseph had the spunk. For I fear Tom called him just about every name in the book before he got up, told me he didn't want to see my so-and-so spoiled baby brother on his property when he got back, and stormed out to do Lord knows what. It was two whole days before Tom came back, unshaven and hungover, to ask if I had any good news to tell him."

"What did you tell him, Miss Flora?"

"That Joseph was gone, of course. A woman's husband has to come first, and I knew the two of them could never dwell under the same roof again after such words had been exchanged. I did give Joseph some money, and he promised to find a means of self-support. That was easier said than done. He joined the army and the rest you know."

Longarm nodded and said, "Then he found out your husband had died and figured you couldn't stand up to him alone. Did you even try, ma'am?"

She nodded grimly and put her broom aside to unbutton her bodice calmly. As Longarm stared in wonder she opened the front of her dress. He tried to ignore her small but perky breasts as he stared at the ugly green and purple bruise marks between them. She said, "Joseph did this when I asked him to leave again a few days ago. You'll have to take my word about where he kicked me after I fell down."

Longarm grimaced. "A man who'd punch a woman so hard would kick her most anywhere, I reckon. Since you brung it up, and I know as a lawman just how ugly family disputes can get, I have another mighty indelicate question I have to ask."

She buttoned back up as she shook her head. "No. He never tried to mistreat me *that* way. I'm not sure he was too interested in *any* girls, and he always hated me when we were growing up together."

He nodded and said, "I'm missing something here, ma'am. From all the testimony you and everyone else seems to agree on, I'll be switched if I can see how come you've been so nice to even a kid brother all these years."

She shrugged. "It wasn't easy. Joseph was always a sullen little brute. But he was *kin*. He had nobody else to turn to after our folk died. I'd just married Tom and he was very sweet about it, until Joseph just stayed on and on, contributing nothing but trouble and an extra mouth to feed."

He'd already heard all that. Longarm said he understood and told her, "I've seen about as much as there could be to see here, ma'am. But before I go, could I have a look at your husband's workshop next door?"

She nodded and got out of his way. "Help yourself. The door's not locked."

Again she remained in the doorway as he entered the larger but, if anything, less cheerful room built in up there. The dusty heads of long-dead critters stared at him from all around. The workbench was cluttered with tools, from meat cleavers to surgeon's clamps, and a bitty library of brown bottles rose above it. Longarm stared at the dismal remains of a half-stuffed jackrabbit and asked, "Would I be safe in assuming your late husband's hobby could have been taxidermy, ma'am?"

"He liked to go hunting on his days off. That was another bone of contention between Tom and my brother. He offered to take Joseph along. Said it might make a man of him. But I guess Joseph preferred reading about Buffalo Bill to acting like Buffalo Bill."

Longarm stared at the not too well mounted pronghorn before he muttered half to himself, "Until *recent*, that is." He could see all too clearly how an older man

24

who fancied himself an outdoorsman, when he got a chance to get outdoors, could feel about a sickly bookworm, content just to read about the West all around them. He picked up some of the jars to read the labels. It sure took a lot of fancy chemicals to put a jackrabbit back on its fool feet after you shot it. He didn't find anything that could turn a sissy into a wild man, even if he could have gotten in here so easily. He asked the brunette if she had any idea as to how her late husband had brought down all these critters, explaining, "I don't see any guns or ammunition around here."

"There might be some spare shells among all Tom's things. His hunting rifle is in the house. Would you like to see it?"

He shook his head. "Not if you know for sure it's still there. As you may have guessed, we're looking for a modest-sized youth packing two pistols but, all right, what sort of rifle bore are we talking about? Would you know?"

She shook her head, then brightened and said, "Oh, I think Tom said it was a thirty something. Is that any help?"

"It is. Nobody around here's been shot with a .30-30 hunting rifle. So there's no need to pester you further."

As they went downstairs together she said, "I'd be happy to show you that rifle, and I still owe you coffee and cake at least."

He turned to her at the bottom of the steps. "Thanks just the same, but I've other calls to make. If you're up to one more dumb question, though, is it at all possible your side of the Slade family could be at all related to the late Black Jack Slade of Julesburg, Colorado?"

She looked blank and said, "We don't have any relation this side of the Mississippi that I know of. Mom and Dad came west from Ohio just before the War. Joseph and I were actually born back in Dayton, but of course we were too little to remember much when they brought us west with them. I guess I was about six or seven and Joseph was about three or four. All I remember is that he cried all the way."

"Then you and him grew up the rest of the way here in Denver and nowheres else?"

She nodded. "I've been up to the mountains with Tom a time or two. I don't think Joseph had ever been out of the city before he joined the army. Why do you ask?"

Longarm said, "He was sure dressed cow for a city boy, the one time I saw him. Would you know where he picked up that outfit?"

She said she didn't. So he ticked his hatbrim to her and left by the alley exit. He knew Denver Dry Goods sold boots, big hats, and gun rigs. But so did a mess of other stores in town, and it would be even hotter down along Larimer Street at this hour. When he got to the end of the alley he headed up the slope in favor of down. By the time he made it up to the more fashionable Sherman Avenue running along the breezier edge of what was in fact the rim of the higher ground surrounding downtown Denver on the South Platte bottomlands he saw he'd made a good move for once. It would have been cooler up here, where the richer folk lived, even if the sandstone walks had not been shaded with elm and cottonwood.

The houses to either side were mostly built with the same red sandstone they'd used for the walks. Rich people seldom got rich by wasting money. So the lawns, while well tended, had been left to turn summer-brown. Come late fall, they'd all get a dressing of manure from the packing houses down by the tracks and, come next spring, they would look nice and green for June weddings and such. But since summer-killed lawns were as delicate as they were ugly, all the neighborhood kids were required to play out on the dusty street and, school being out, they were. It wasn't true that kids who got to eat regular were sissies. The ones down the avenue just ahead were playing ball in the street as if it was a cooler day and they'd never heard about carriage traffic. As he crossed an intersection, Longarm saw a ball coming his way. Since he'd been a kid once, too, he bent to stop it, lest it wind up somewhere in Cheyenne.

As he caught the bounding ball a bullet grazed his bent-over spine, hit his hatbrim, and took his Stetson off for him. He dove headfirst, landed on the back of his neck, and somersaulted back to his boot heels to make some sudden moves. The kids had to come first. He threw the ball as hard as he could. It passed over them, catty-corner, to roll across a forbidden lawn as the kids, being kids, chased it out of the line of fire.

By this time Longarm was behind the solid trunk of a good old elm and he was glad he was when he heard a second distant shot, a rooster laugh, and the bullet slamming into the far side of the trunk. It hit hard enough for a .45 round. He cursed and got his own .44-40 out to return the courtesy. But as he risked a peek he saw the only moving target back that way was a uniformed roundsman running his way with police whistle chirping and nightstick waving. Longarm cursed again, put his sidearm back in its cross-draw holster, and stepped into view, hands polite.

The copper badge recognized him, slowed to a wary walk, and called out, "I just heard gunshots up this way, Longarm."

"It wasn't me. You must have passed the son of a bitch just now. How come?" Longarm asked.

The uniformed lawman said, "I didn't pass nobody, save for some kids running for home as their mothers was yelling at 'em to do this instant. Who was shooting at whom, and why?"

Longarm looked the other way and, sure enough, the kids whose ball he'd stopped were out of sight, too. Rich folk were careful about their kids as well as their money, having got that way by being less casual about whatever they owned, most likely. He told the copper badge, "Some son of a bitch just pegged two shots at me. I'd say he was wearing hair chaps and a big black sombrero if I didn't respect a fellow lawman's vision so much. The rascal is little enough to pass for a running kid at a casual glance, if he was wearing a tamer outfit. You might not have spied him at all if he worked his way to wherever between two houses. Picket-fence lines and even hedges don't seem as fashionable up here along the avenue."

The roundsman said, "I've noticed that. It makes life hard on me on Halloween. You'd think a man with the money for a sixty- or seventy-foot lot would want to fence it. But most don't, and the little shits run every which way after they kick over an ash can. How do you feel about the shootist firing on you from, say, any one of them houses, themselves?"

"I'd feel surprised as hell. Both shots came my way fired level. Ain't a porch in sight that ain't well above the grade. Aside from that, I don't think the cuss who was shooting at me would be socially acceptable up here on Sherman Avenue. I know *I* ain't."

The copper badge got out his notepad and asked Longarm to try for some names. Longarm said, "It works more ways than one. Working as long as I have for the department, a man picks up an occasional enemy. As I hardly have to tell *you*, only a few of the rascals we arrest really mean it when they promise to look us up when they get out. But now and again one does. It seems more likely, as I study on it, that I just saved myself a needless train ride to Julesburg, though."

He brought the roundsman up to date on Joseph, alias Black Jack, Slade as they both stepped out into the intersection to rescue Longarm's hat. He picked it up, dusted it off, and put it on again as the Denver lawman opined, "He won't last long with that sort of attitude. He must be crazy."

28

Longarm said, "That's what makes him so dangerous. And, no offense, he ain't been caught yet, with every lawman in the city out to catch him."

The roundsman wanted Longarm to come to the precinct house with him to make a statement. Longarm shook his head. "There's nothing to report. I ain't hurt. He could be most anywhere in town by now. This ain't shaping up as a paperwork case. We've already got all sorts of stuff about young Slade on paper, and none of it helps. He's gone loco. He ain't acting at all like the sissy weakling everyone's always known. He's acting like he's turned into someone else entire. He may think he really has. So keep your eye peeled for a mousy-looking little shrimp as has suddenly took to acting like one of the wildest killers the West has ever seen."

As he shook with the copper badge and ambled on, Longarm mused aloud to himself, "I'm sure glad the one and original Black Jack Slade is dead and buried. I'd hate like hell to go up against *two* such dangerous lunatics at once!"

Chapter 3

Mavis Weatherwax was not a widow woman. She was a divorcee. Some said her former husband had settled a silver mine on her in exchange for her promise never to speak to him again. Her big bay-windowed house stood close to the capitol grounds, where they cut Sherman Avenue in twain. When she came to the door herself, Longarm sensed she'd given her servants the weekend off and had not been expecting company. The junoesque henna-rinsed divorcee had her red hair pinned up properly, but she wore nothing more than a green silk kimono over her considerable curves.

She told him he was a pleasant surprise and asked what she owed for the pleasure. They both knew he hadn't come for one of the piano lessons she was in the habit of giving. Longarm didn't know why a gal with her own income wanted to give piano lessons in the first place. The lady who had introduced them at a party a spell back had said Mavis found it a handy excuse to meet young fellows, but some women were inclined to say spiteful things about any gal who was halfway decent-looking and free to do the things *they* couldn't.

Longarm told her, "I got some sheet music I'd like an expert opinion on, Miss Mavis. I can't read music much beyond a hymn book but there's something odd going on here, unless I've forgotten Sunday School entire."

She hauled him inside and said she was ever ready to cooperate with the law. The powder and paint she wore looked softer inside, but her French perfume smelled stronger. She led him into her parlor, where a Steinway grand was corralled in the bay window, taking up most of the space. He handed her the "Ballad of Black Jack Slade." She blinked at the cover and said, "Good heavens," and slid her heroic silk-sheathed behind in place behind the keyboard. She patted what was left of the piano bench for him to sit beside her. He took her up on her invitation and, even sitting closer to her than some might consider proper, he had to let some of his own rump hang over the edge.

She didn't seem to notice his hip against her own as she put the sheet music on the piano rack and commenced to thump away. She sang the words as well, not badly at all, although they sure sounded silly coming from a lady with such a high-toned contralto.

He stopped her when she got to the bottom of the first page and said, "That's enough for now. The last time I heard this song sung it was sung to a different tune. I don't play the piano any better than I play the typewriter, but let me see if I can one-finger the way it went last night in less seemly surroundings."

She listened as he tried to reproduce the more dismal way the wanted man had sounded off in the Parthenon until she decided, "You're flat. I think I know that tune. It's an old Irish jig, and it goes like this."

He listened as she tinkled a few bars. Then he said, "Well, he must have been flat, too, but that's about the way it sounded last night. How come you say it's an

32

Irish jig? Slade ain't an Irish name, is it?"

"I think it's an old Saxon name. That's not the point. Half our so-called cowboy songs are based on Irish, German, or old English folk songs. You could hardly expect a semi-literate with a poetic streak to compose original *music* as well. Is there any point to this discussion, Custis? By either melody, this attempt at a ballad is pretty awful."

He said, "You've helped me a heap, Miss Mavis. For now I know two things I didn't know for sure before. I am looking for a kid who don't read music and just admired the words of that song about his hero. Better yet, I know he never learned it riding with other cowhands, for had he done so, he'd have known the tune and not just one he'd heard in his modest travels."

She leaned closer and told him, sort of sultry, that she had no idea what on earth he was talking about.

He figured he owed her that much for her help. So he commenced to bring her up to date on the crazy case he was working on. She had somehow herded them both over to a purple plush sofa across the room before he was halfway through, and though he hadn't invited her to snuggle against him so close it didn't hurt, and he was recovering from the first shock of her perfume. He had an interesting view down the open V of her loosely tied kimono as well, and he was beginning to suspect he was supposed to. But she must have felt she'd make him nervous if she moved in on him any faster, which was true, so she said, "My, that poor boy does sound strange. But what good does it do you to know he's devoid of any musical talent as well as common sense, Custis?"

He caught his arm about to slip off the back of the sofa behind her, warned it to behave itself, and said, "The kid has never met anyone who knew the real Black Jack Slade well enough to sing about him. He memorized the words of that ballad, likely reading them over

33

and over in his lonely room, until he had them down pat, even if he had the tune wrong."

She repressed a yawn. "Oh, this warm weather makes me so drowsy! Do you mind if I rest my head on your shoulder like this? Go ahead, I'm all ears. Tell me some more about the Wild West."

He figured he'd better. The widow woman who'd introduced him to this enthusiastic listener had warned him she'd feed his heart to the hawks if he ever went near her and, right now, he was so near her it was starting to make him tingle where he knew he'd promised not to. He said, "I told you young Joe Slade had just about every penny dreadful ever printed about real and made-up desperate characters. I found stories about Buffalo Bill, Wild Bill, Billy the Kid, and a female bandit named Billie Bangs. I don't think she could be real. I didn't find one fuller account of the notorious Black Jack Slade, and I know more than one such story has been published. I've seen 'em on many a news-stand."

She shrugged or nestled closer, it was hard to tell, and said, "You found the sheet music he'd bought. Maybe that was all he had to know about the dreadful man."

Longarm shook his head. "I don't think so. Once he'd memorized that simple-minded song he didn't need to look at it no more. But I think he took a longer printed account of the one and original Black Jack Slade *with* him. Are you aware of where your hand is resting at the moment, ma'am?"

She giggled. "I am. Aren't you? Go on. Why would he want to carry around a pulp penny dreadful about the real Jack Slade?"

"As a Bible. Anyone who's so tired of being his puny original self that he's convinced his fool self he's some-body *else* might want written directions as to his new, proper conduct. If I knew which of the many versions of the story he was using for his research I'd have a chance of outguessing the mean little brute. But so many have been written since the real Black Jack was lynched, years ago, that his would-be second coming could be out to do wonders that never happened, and . . . Madam, are you aware that what you're doing with your head in my lap is a violation of the criminal statutes of the state of Colorado?"

She didn't answer. She must have thought it impolite to talk with her mouth full. Longarm stared down at her bobbing red head with ever growing fondness and reflected that he was, after all, a *federal* lawman, and that Colorado could worry about its own dumb laws. The widow woman down the avenue who'd introduced him to this literal man-eater was going to cry fire and salt if she ever found out about this, and the odds were fifty-fifty she would, since women could brag as bad as men about such matters. On the other hand, *this* one was sure to say even *meaner* things about him if he tried to stop her at this late date, and what man born of mortal clay was about to stop at a time like this, in any case?

So they both went deliciously crazy for a spell, and Longarm was only mildly surprised, when they stopped for breath at last, to find himself bare-ass under the piano with her smiling up at him adoringly, with her bare feet pressed against the bottom of the sounding board. He'd been wondering what those funny harpish drummings he'd been hearing were. They sure had a fine grip on one another with her wide-spread heels braced that way.

He kissed her some more and said, "Well, howdy, pard. I was *wondering* where *you* might be whilst I was up in heaven. But don't you have a bed on the premises?"

She sounded serious as she demurely replied, "Oh,

never. That would be downright *indecent*, Custis! Whatever would you think of me if I went to bed with you in broad daylight?"

"I'd think you were being practical about splinters in your sweet bare behind. This is a sort of silly place to screw, no offense."

"None taken. I'm lying on my kimono, if you must know. I like a firm surface under me when you thrust so hard. It makes it *feel* so hard."

He noticed that as he moved experimentally in her, but she said, "Wait. I do think my tailbone's getting bruised. Let's try it a more comfortable way, dear."

He said he was willing to try anything that didn't hurt. So they crawled out from under the piano to try it on the rug with her on top. He found that was inspirational indeed. As she moved up and down atop him he judged her waistline to measure no more than twenty-odd inches, without a lick of whalebone or India rubber to help, and her heroic breasts bounced proud and firm in defiance of the laws of gravity.

It felt so good he would have been content to do it some more, but she said, "We have to think of my reputation," and popped off him to add, "Come on. The neighbors have big ears."

He had no idea what she was talking about as she led him back over to the piano. She lowered the big lid and climbed atop the bed-sized instrument, patting the black varnish beside her naked flesh as she asked him what he was waiting for.

He said, "I ain't waiting for anything. I'm trying to figure out what you want me to do."

"You've been in here almost an hour. They've only heard the piano play a few bars, quite a while ago. Would that sound like a music lesson to you, if you were an old biddy hen?"

He said he doubted it and, grasping her intent at last, got aboard the piano with her. The hard, slippery surface felt odd against his bare flesh. It felt even odder, albeit good, when he mounted her big, soft body again and she raised her hands over her head to reach down to the keyboard and moan, "Faster!" as she proceded to play "Kitten on the Keys."

He laughed like hell and did his best to keep in time with her as she tinkled and bounced her bare bottom at the same time. He hoped her nosy neighbors thought she had a big bass drum in here as well, for it sure sounded like it.

After climaxing again together in such an artistic fashion, they both lay quietly in each other's arms for a spell. Then she sighed and said, "That was lovely. But it's getting late, darling. They have to see you leaving before suppertime."

He'd been hoping against hope she was going to let him escape without the tears and recriminations a man who enjoyed life just had to accept with the nicer words of womankind. So he kissed her fondly and said, "Yeah, we wouldn't want 'em to think we've been nibbling on each other."

She laughed low and dirty, but shoved him off, and damned near broke his neck as he rolled off the piano as well.

It only took her a moment to climb back into her kimono. As she sat on the sofa beside him, watching him dress, she sighed and told him, "Lord have mercy, but we can't go on like this, Custis."

He hadn't been planning to, but he thought it only decent to look wistful and say, "I know. I ought to be whipped with snakes for taking advantage of a sweet little helpless thing like you."

She nodded. "I don't think any of the bruises will show, but you're right. I just can't resist you. That's why you're going to have to be brave for *both* of us, darling."

He tried to sound heartbroken as he asked, "Does

that mean you don't want me coming back no more, Miss Mavis?"

She said, "I want you so bad I can taste it, even after coming all those times just now. But I have to consider my good name, and you know how everyone gossips about a divorced woman."

He nodded. "Yeah, it seems mean as hell. For it only stands to reason most married gals get screwed more regular than even the wildest divorcee."

"You don't know how true that *is*, darling. You may have noticed I was feeling sort of frustrated when you surprised me this afternoon. You can't do that again. People are sure to talk as it is. But I've an idea. Where will you be going when you leave here?"

"I ain't sure. You sort of surprised me, too. I had a doctor I wanted to consult about demented bookworms and the public library might have more than a song about Black Jack Slade on hand. But they'd both be closed by the time I could get to either, now. So I reckon I'll have me some supper and just prowl about some more."

"Oh, I was thinking, if you knew a very, very discreet little love nest we could sort of get to separately and discreet . . ."

"I'd sure like that," he lied, "but I'm on the trail of a mad-dog killer and he just showed me there's no place in town that's safe. I dare not risk your pretty hide, Miss Mavis. My own could be in enough trouble if he spots me before I spot him again."

He got to his feet, buckling his gun rig, and put on his hat to leave. As he did so she rose beside him, grabbed him around the waist, and hugged him close as she said, "Oh, dear, if you're really in *that* much danger you'd better stay here after all. I'd rather risk my reputation than let you risk your life, you sweet man."

"That would be wrong for both of us, little darling," he told her. "No man who has to look at his fool self in the mirror when he's shaving could ask a lady to get ruined for him. And, besides, I don't see how I'd ever catch that killer under your piano. So I'd best get it on down the road."

As he was leaving she coyly suggested her bed might not be too improper a place to explore, after dark. But he left anyway, before she could set a date for his next music lesson.

As he moved on down the avenue under the shade trees a little old lady wearing a sunbonnet was sweeping her front walk. When he ticked his hatbrim at her, she smiled and said, "Isn't it nice out this evening, now that it's started to cool off?"

He smiled back and said, "Yes, ma'am. It sure is a lot cooler than it was just a short spell ago."

Chapter 4

The Denver Public Library wasn't the only place in town a man could find a book. A little used bookstore on Larimer was open despite the hour. It smelled dusty inside. A little bearded gent wearing specs and a skullcap came out from the back to ask what he could do for the only customer in sight.

Longarm said, "I see you mostly sell regular books, and I don't blame you. But I'm looking for a Wild West magazine about a real albeit unlikely gent named Black Jack Slade."

The old book dealer looked pained. "Books about how to build a steam engine or rescue a maiden from a dragon are not good enough for you? We got books of fact and fiction. We got books old and new. We got books by Sir Walter Scott and books by authors nobody ever heard of and probably shouldn't. But a book about a *black jackal?* I don't think so."

Longarm said he was sorry for being such a pest and turned to go. But the old man stopped him. "Wait. You say you want a penny dreadful? Them we got. Come, I'll show you. We got a couple of boxes of such trash as part of a house-cleaning sale a few days ago. I was saving them for the rag picker, but who knows?"

Longarm followed the old man back through the musty racks, then through a curtained doorway into pitch blackness. The old man struck a match to light a wall lamp. They were in a small, cluttered storage space piled floor-to-ceiling with pasteboard boxes and wooden crates. The old man hauled a battered child's toy box out into the light and opened the lid, saying, "Look and enjoy. I'll be out front if you find anything."

Longarm hunkered down, setting the top layers of mouldering cheap paper neatly aside until, halfway to the bottom, he found a once-garish, now-faded cover that still looked mighty wild. He read the date—November, 1866—and set the old magazine aside until he'd replaced the others, closed the lid, and shoved the box back where it belonged. Then he picked up his treasure, put the lamp out, and rejoined the old man near the front of the shop.

"I'll take this one, sir. How much do I owe you?" he asked.

The old man shrugged. "Take it. I sell *books*, not wastepaper. I told you I was going to get rid of all that trash. I've been meaning to put it out back in the alley, but my son is away on business and my back is not what it used to be."

Longarm said, "You have to let me pay you. This has to be one of the earliest pulp books about a real person, so some of it could be based on fact. You see, I ain't a gent with bad taste in literature. I'm a deputy U.S. marshal, and this dumb old penny dreadful could be serious evidence in a murder case."

The old man laughed incredulously and said, "Where but in America could such things happen? You need the book, take the book. It's one less I have to carry out with my aching back."

"Now, look, the cover says it sold for a nickel back in Sixty-six. What say we settle for that, at least?"

The old man shook his head stubbornly. "I'm an ethical businessman. I don't cheat customers. I got that whole box of old magazines thrown in, *free,* as part of the deal I made for a couple of hundred *real* books I really *wanted.* How could I charge you for something I never paid for and was just going to throw out? It's against the law to do a small favor for a lawman?"

Longarm said, "You sure are a stubborn old cuss, no offense. But would you agree one good turn deserves another?"

The old man shrugged. "Do me a favor and we'll call it square."

Longarm took off his hat and coat, put them on the counter with the favor the old man had just done him, and said, "All right. You show me where you want things piled, and that's where I'll pile 'em for you."

"You don't mean that," the old man replied. "I got at least a ton of scrap paper to leave out back for the rag picker."

"We'd better get cracking, then," Longarm said.

Longarm didn't think it made much sense, either, by the time they'd finished. The spry old man had done some of the work, of course, so they were both paper-dusty by the time they'd toted all the trash books the old man was too proud to sell out to the alley. As he dropped the last heavy box beside the back gate, Longarm said, "I hope nobody steals all this paper before your pal can pick it up."

"Let them," the old man said. "Anyone willing to lift such a load deserves it. We both must be crazy, but for a lawman you're a nice change. Where I come from, lawmen don't help an honest merchant. They help themselves to his merchandise. Do you like sweet wine? I got sweet wine inside and we've agreed one good turn deserves another."

Longarm grinned, wiped his sweaty face with his pocket kerchief, and said, "We're going to have to stop doing favors for each other before we both wind up crippled. Are we square about that old magazine now?"

"Idiot, I told you it was yours to begin with. But I thank you just the same. I can't wait to write my brother in the old country that *here* the cossacks are harmless lunatics."

They went back inside. Longarm gathered up his things and they parted friendly. The balmy dry air of the mile-high city dried him off as it cooled him down. But the combined effects of a hundred and thirty pound gal and a ton or so of less interesting stuff to manhandle had left him feeling exhausted and thirsty. So when he came to a neighborhood saloon, as sedate as such things got, along Larimer, he ducked in to settle his nerves and catch up on his reading.

The place was laid out a lot like Luke Short's Long Branch in Dodge. Built into a storefront, it was no more than twenty feet wide and ran back about forty. The bar ran the long way, along one wall. Small tables were set along the other wall. The place was almost empty, save for a few regulars and a desperate as well as homely Mex gal lounging against the bar in a flouncy skirt with an organdy rose pinned to one overweight hip. As he ordered a schooner of needled beer at the bar she flashed a gold tooth at him and murmured, *"Buenoches, querido. A 'onde va?"*

He was going to a table to sit down. He didn't answer her with more than a dry smile. As he moved to do so, she started to follow, but the barkeep warned her in Spanish that she was messing with the law. Sometimes it came in handy to be so well known in the rougher parts of town, Longarm thought.

He sat at a table facing the front, drank some suds, and spread his find on the table. It was entitled, "Black Jack Slade, Terror of the Overland Trail."

So far so accurate.

The Overland Trail, like a lot of stagecoach trails, had more or less died with the coming of the Iron Horse. Rails now ran along parts of it. Other parts were still used as wagon traces by local traffic. Some had just been allowed to go back to seed, mostly tumbleweed. The old Overland Trail didn't interest Longarm as much as the wild-eyed rascals who'd haunted it back in the transcontinental stagecoach era, and as he read the book, he had to allow the writer had tried to get some of the facts Longarm already knew right. So it was safe to assume some of the things Longarm *didn't* know could be based on yarns still fresh at the time of publication.

Trying to make old Black Jack out a misunderstood Robin Hood was silly, of course. Slade had started out decent enough with an honorable discharge after the Mexican War and been hired as a supervisor by the Central Overland California & Pikes Peak Express Company, posted at Julesburg, where the stage lines forked to serve both the older mining camps out California way and the new Colorado strikes between Pikes Peak and Cherry Creek, as Denver had been called at the time. So he'd had a good job, had he had sense to behave right. Suffering snakes! His name had not started out as Black Jack. He'd been hired as *Joseph* Slade by Overland, and it was no wonder a half-cracked little bookworm had been struck by the fact they were *both* baptized the very same way!

Longarm read on about the Terror of the Overland Trail, and old Black Jack Slade had surely been that. He began his job for Overland by commencing to fuss with a French-Canadian fellow supervisor named Bené. The book said Bené was a dishonest employee who'd been robbing the company. It was a mite late to ask why

Overland hadn't just fired Bené, in that case. The mutual admiration between Slade and Bené had been settled by Bené shooting Slade first, a lot, making the mistake of leaving Slade alive, and winding up with his tanned ear dangling from old Black Jack's watch chain.

Most gents would have stopped right there. Having established his rep as a mighty grim man to cross, Black Jack took to scaring folk just for practice. Within three years he was getting too famous to stay alive much longer in Julesburg, so he'd crossed into Montana with a Colorado warrant out on him.

He and his long-suffering wife settled down in Montana to raise cows and hell. There was no mention of them having any kids, so there went any hope of the latter-day Slade having any basis for his delusion. The original Black Jack hailed from Illinois, not Ohio. No matter how the writer tried to justify the original model as a misunderstood hero, Longarm could see he should have stayed in Julesburg, where at least folk were scared of him. Acting crazy-mean hadn't worked so good in the Montana mining country around Virginia City. The local vigilance committee advised Black Jack politely to saddle up and ride far. He took this as an invitation to indulge in a week-long drunk and shooting spree the vigilantes didn't find half as amusing. So they found a rope and a handy beef-loading scaffold in the Virginia City yards and hung him up to cool considerable. The sad tale ended with old Black Jack buried in Salt Lake City, Utah. The reasons given made no sense at all to Longarm. But then, nothing *either* Black Jack Slade had done made much sense.

He was going over that part again, sure it had to be a mistake, when two mistakes took place in the here and now in rapid succession. The homely Mex gal at the bar stepped away from it for another try at his virtue just as someone who had to like him less fired at Longarm through the window from outside.

The gal and a lot of busted glass went down as Longarm leaped up, gun in hand, to fire back as he charged. The sill of the shattered window stood two feet above the floor. Longarm leaped over it to land with both boot heels on something softer than he'd expected Larimer to be paved with. He fired straight down as he bounced off and put another round in the son of a bitch for good measure. Then he saw he was wasting ammunition and hunkered down by a watering trough to reload as he swept the rapidly clearing street with his narrowed eyes. He saw that nobody else seemed to want any part of the action. The only possible targets headed his way were waving police nightsticks, so he got to his feet and holstered his gun before they could make any mistakes about *him*.

One of the local lawmen shouted, "What's this all about, cowboy? Oh, it's you, Longarm. We might have known. Do you always have to act like it's the Fourth of July?"

Longarm pointed at the body stretched out on the walk between them and said, "It was *his* grand notion, not mine. Hold the fort. There's another one down inside."

He ran back into the saloon. The only soul in sight was the Mex gal on the floor. He bent to help her. She was smiling up at him sort of confused, but he knew she wasn't really seeing anything. He closed her eyes with gentle fingers and lowered her head back to the floor.

As he got back to his feet one of the copper badges came in to say, "It sure is easy to draw a crowd in this part of town, but my pard can no doubt keep anyone from stealing that other gent's boots before the meat wagon shows up. Oh, I see you shot old Mexican Martha as well. Any particular reason, Longarm?"

Longarm said, "I didn't know her. She was trying to know me better and got in the line of fire. She took a round meant for *me,* and I ought to be stood in the corner for sitting in view from the street outside after dark."

As they moved back toward the open entrance, the barkeep rose from behind his bar to ask who was going to pay for his front window. Neither lawman answered. The Denver officer said, "He must have wanted you bad. Was he the killer they told us you all were looking for? No offense, but he don't fit the description too good."

Longarm stared morosely down at the taller, older man dressed in faded denim. "His name was Edward Morrison. They called him Texas Teddy. I put him away some years ago for stealing army supplies. He swore at the time he'd pay me back, and I reckon he must have meant it."

One of the copper badges said, "He should have quit whilst he was ahead. One can see by his prison pallor that he ain't been out long. Now he's going to serve even more time, *underground*. Do you reckon he's the one as fired on you earlier today? We heard about that, coming on duty just a while ago. The duty sergeant told us to watch for that bitty gent in goat-hair chaps, though."

Longarm said, "I was watching for him, too. That's why I thought it safe to let my guard down on a well-lit street, if I was thinking at all, cuss my careless brains."

"You know, of course, that the county coroner will expect even a gent like you to show up for the hearing, don't you?" one of the officers asked.

Longarm nodded. "My office is my mailing address, and you got it on file," he told them. "I wish real life worked the way it does in penny-dreadful shootouts. I hate it when they ask so many dumb questions."

"You think *you* got troubles, Longarm. We have to fill out all sorts of papers every time we bring in anybody."

Longarm grimaced and went back inside. The scene

was the same. He put some money on the bar and told the barkeep, "I want you to use this to see she's buried decent. I can't afford nothing fancy, but she deserves better than a scrap of canvas and a hole in potter's field, savvy?"

The barkeep scooped up the gold coins and said, "I know an old Mex who'll build a pine box and work something out with the sexton at the church of Santa Catalina across the creek. What the priest don't know about old Martha won't hurt him. But who's going to pay for my front window?"

"I didn't bust it. But I will, after I see you haven't played me and this lady false. Make sure every dime I just gave you is spent honest on her burial and come next payday I'll be by to talk about your glass. But if I find out she wound up in potter's field—and I *can*, easy—you can commend your soul to Jesus, for your ass and everything else in here will be busted up by *me*."

The barkeep assured Longarm he had no intention of crossing anyone who shot so good. So Longarm went back outside to watch them load the other body in the wagon. He told them the one inside was personal property. They said they didn't care, since it saved space in an already overcrowded city plot. As the wagon rolled away, Longarm saw Sergeant Nolan crossing Larimer to join him. He said, "I know, I know, I *said* I'd fill out all the damned papers for Denver, damn it."

Nolan said, "That can wait. That ain't what I come looking to tell you. Your Black Jack Slade has struck again and, since this time it's outside the city limits, the captain says to tell you the crazy little owlhoot is all Uncle Sam's. For he just shot up an army post, way to the northeast, and it was a well known fact he disliked the army even *before* he gunned them military police last night."

Longarm frowned thoughtfully and said, "Damn, I

thought that penny dreadful left something out. By any chance did the more recent Black Jack Slade raise all this ned anywhere near Fort Halleck on the old Overland Trail?"

"He didn't shoot up anything *near* Fort Halleck," Nolan said. "He was right on the post when he tore into the canteen, to demand a drink, and then shot up a couple of troopers and all the lights, when they refused him service. How did you know it was Fort Halleck, though?"

Longarm said, "I just remembered. The original Black Jack had to run for Montana after he shot up Fort Halleck in Sixty-one. That wasn't heroic enough to put in a story trying to make a trigger-happy killer look sensible, but it happened anyway."

"Well, history sure seems to be repeating itself of late, don't you think?" Nolan said.

Longarm said, "I don't think. I *know*. That crazy young owlhoot is following in the footsteps of his idol, guns and all!"

Chapter 5

"I heard. Why are you still here in Denver?" asked Marshal Vail as his calmer wife showed Longarm into the sitting room of their residence atop Capital Hill.

Longarm noted the yellow telegram on the lamp table next to Vail's easy chair. "That's what I came to clear with you. I just had to shoot Texas Teddy Morrison. That didn't take half as long as all the fool paperwork at police headquarters. They say they don't blame me for swatting such a fly, but that I can't leave town until after the coroner's jury clears me."

Vail said, "Sure you can. Texas Teddy had a Kansas warrant out on him, and never should have come to Colorado in the first place. I get my hair cut in the same barbershop as the coroner, and he ain't all that stupid. Did you give them a deposition stating all you care to know about Texas Teddy's demise?"

Longarm said, "I did. In triplicate. All three copies signed and witnessed."

"There you go," Vail said. "I'll chip in my own statement under a federal letterhead, saying I sent you out in the field on more serious business, and that ought to do 'em. I see you just missed the last northbound this side of sunrise. So why don't you just trot on down the avenue and ask that widow woman you sleep with to set her alarm for you?"

Mrs. Vail, who knew the lady in question socially, and didn't enjoy gossip as much as her husband did, gasped in dismay and left the room. Longarm sat down across from Vail and said, "That was spiteful, Billy. Do I tell *you* who to sleep with?"

Vail sighed. "There *was* a time, but lately it hardly seems worth all the suspense. I don't know if I'm getting old or getting smart. But had I known that shapesome lass just down the way felt so lonely I might have beat you to her."

Longarm got out a smoke. "Can we stop dreaming and get back to *another* idjet's dream world? I'm going to need extra expenses on this job, if we're in a race with the War Department. I can't ask for the loan of an army mount at Fort Halleck if old Colonel Walthers is mad at us."

Vail nodded. "Get a livery nag at Julesburg when your train stops there and we'll wire the money if the price sounds right. You'll do better owning the horse instead of hiring it if you mean to follow the Overland Trail. As I recall, it stretched from Council Bluffs to Sacramento in its day."

"With side branches," Longarm agreed, "but I doubt even a lunatic would be out to haunt all of it. The kid's fixation on Black Jack Slade ought to confine his sleepwalking to the parts his hero raised hell on. But you're right about my needing a bought and paid for mount and maybe a pack animal. We are discussing anywhere between Julesburg and Salt Lake, with a side trip up into the Montana mining country, where the Overland stage never went but Black Jack did."

Vail nodded but said, "I know he got lynched in Virginia City because I read about it at the time. I don't recall him getting in trouble as far west as Utah, though."

"That's where he's buried, on paper," Longarm said. "I mean to look into that some more if ever I can find an account that makes sense. Who do you reckon would have all the properly kept records on that old case on file, Billy?"

Vail said flatly, "Nobody. Conditions out this way was more casual before the War. I was riding with the Rangers at the time. We was sort of overworked, so we only wrote down serious stuff, like another Comanche rising. I doubt the vigilance committee that strung Black Jack Slade up paid half as much attention as us Rangers to pencil pushing. As to other papers out on him at the time he done the rope dance, they'd be filed hither and yon along the wake of his wanderings. Sedgwick County might have records of his more dastardly doings in Julesburg. He had to go through Wyoming to wind up dead in Montana and he always made trouble everywhere he stopped for a drink. I still can't see why he had to go to Utah afterwards."

Longarm said, "Neither can I. The version I just read says that after he was cut down his long-suffering wife, Virginia, had him salted and boxed so's she could carry him home to Carlyle, Illinois, with his kin. Only it was summer, and they hadn't used near enough salt. So by the time they got to Salt Lake he just had to be buried, sudden, and the Latter-Day Saints were kind enough to provide a plot."

Vail frowned and said, "Something's rotten in Denmark, and I don't mean that licorice whip you just lit. Don't it strike you odd that a man lynched in Virginia City would have a wife named Virginia dumb enough to bury him in Utah on the way to Illinois from Montana?"

"I've noticed a lot of penny dreadful writers do get

their geography a mite mixed up. I reckon the gent who had to fluff out the bare-bones account enough to fill all them pages didn't know Montana lies northeast, not west, of Salt Lake City, and he had to give Slade's wife *some* damn name. I can check out a friendly Mormon elder I know. They couldn't have buried a Gentile in any of their cemeteries without noticing, and they're great ones for keeping records."

Vail reached for a defensive cigar in his own humidor and bit off the end before he growled, "In that case, why are we mulling over such petty details? Even if the original Black Jack could still be alive, he'd be a grown man about my age, not a sassy little runt in his early twenties."

Longarm explained, "Black Jack Junior, as I feel it handy to think of him, don't seem to know that. He's been acting as if he thinks he's the real thing and, if he read how mysterious the final disposition of any body at all seem to be, it could stand to reason, in his unreasonable mind, that Black Jack, meaning him, somehow survived that lynching, and so now he's *back,* see?"

Vail lit his cigar before he shook out the match. "No, I don't. Vigilante hangings tended to be crude, but the result was usually fatal, anyhow."

Longarm insisted, "None of us were there. Slade did live through a fusillade of pistol shots and shotgun blasts that time, and old Roy Bean down on the Pecos is always bragging about the time *he* got strung up by vigilantes and survived."

Vail snorted in disgust. "That old windbag couldn't tell the truth if it was in his favor. He don't like to admit his stiff neck is from old age, so he made up a whopper to excuse it. I have never seen such a country for whopping, and I been out here all my life."

Longarm nodded. "That's my point. Black Jack Junior is living a tall tale. It's like them other lunatics who insist they are the one and original Napoleon, even if they can't speak a word of French or tell you where Waterloo might be. To track the rascal down, I have to know what he *thinks* his new self did in the past or might do in the future. So when I hand in my expenses on this case, I don't want you fussing me about all the Wild West magazines you may find charged to the Department."

Vail scowled and growled, "The hell you say. I have to justify such purchases to the accounting office."

"I'll put down five to fifty cents for an item called research material and it'll be our little secret," Longarm insisted. "I know he's packing at least one magazine I ain't come across yet, because there was nothing in that sheet music or the old account I found this evening about the time Black Jack shot up Fort Halleck. I only remembered, after his young namesake done it, that I'd heard the tale one time as I was waiting to change trains up that way. If I could come by the exact issue he seems to be following, I'd be in a position to head him off instead of just waiting to learn what he'd done next, see?"

Vail did, but he had to say, "I'm sorry I didn't stick to my original disinclination and let the infernal army track him."

"Do you really think old Colonel Walthers could do it, boss?"

"That puffed up blue-belly couldn't track anything. I told you I wanted you to bring in that young killer, not to keep me up past my bedtime discussing his mental state. So get out of here and let me get to bed. Just thinking about you and that handsome young widow woman down the avenue has suddenly inspired me to turn in early, if I can inspire anyone else around here to forget about darning my socks. I can't think of anything less interesting than darning socks. So let's both call it a day, hear?"

* * *

Longarm had more than one good reason not to take Billy Vail's indelicate suggestion about the young widow woman just down Sherman Avenue. It was tempting, despite his earlier music lesson, but he knew she'd start by fussing at him for showing up on her doorstep so late, and he'd have a hell of a time getting any sleep before he'd convinced her that, no, he *wasn't* using her as any port in a storm after another and no doubt younger gal had turned him down. He was really tired, and he had an early train to catch. So he headed for his own furnished digs, closer to the Union Depot. He chuckled fondly as he recalled the time he'd told the widow woman his landlady was the only true port in the storm he ever took advantage of. For she'd almost brained him with a chamber pot before he convinced her his landlady was older than both of them put together.

He chuckled some more as he strode down the steep slope to Lincoln, digging in his boot heels to keep from getting there faster than he wanted to. He knew that if he cut to his right and kept following Lincoln it would take him to the scene of an ugly shootout and the pretty Flora Banes. He wondered why such a notion had crossed his mind as he kept going straight. He'd just told himself a few hours in bed alone wouldn't hurt too bad, and if there was one pretty gal in town he'd have a time bedding down with it had to be Flora Banes. For no matter how she might feel about her baby brother, she could hardly be panting with desire for any lawman out to bring the mean little cuss to justice. The house would no doubt be staked out by other lawmen by now, in any case. Flora's brother sure knew how to make himself popular.

He crossed Broadway and strode through the shabbier, less well-lamped wedge of small businesses and low-rent housing beyond, until he got to Cherry Creek. There was a plank bridge about a quarter of a mile out of his way, but in high summer Cherry Creek ran so dry that one could ford it dry-shod by hopping from one sandbar to another. The schoolkids of Denver did it all the time for fun. It was considered sissy for a kid to take off his or her shoes or socks, and dangerous to step in any of the places water ran mere inches deep. For it was widely accepted that the wide but almost dry watercourse was filled with quicksand, as well as placergold, of course.

The moon was high. Longarm made it across as good as any ten-year-old could have, and followed a cinder path to his rooming house.

No lights were showing in the front windows. He wasn't surprised. His old landlady could spy on the world late at night better with her bedroom lamp out and her lace curtains closed. He waved up at her, anyway, and let himself in. He went upstairs to his own corner room and felt automatically for the match stem that should have been wedged into the jamb above the top hinge.

It wasn't there. A man had to stop and study on a thing like that. It wasn't cleaning day and, in any case, he'd trained the cleaning girl to put that match stem back in place after she'd dusted his seldom-used room once or twice a week. For there'd have been no sense in taking the precaution if it hadn't been meant to inform him that someone had opened his door without his invitation.

The late Texas Teddy hadn't been the only moody gent an ace deputy marshal had annoyed in six or eight years riding for the Justice Department. While Black Jack Junior had to be a good hundred and fifty miles to the northeast this evening, Longarm still drew his .44-40, took a deep breath, and busted in low and crabbing to one side, ready for almost anything but what was seated on his bed with the lamp lit.

57

Flora Banes gasped and jumped up as Longarm rose, gun muzzle more polite, to say, "Howdy, ma'am. Don't ever do that again."

"Your landlady said she didn't think you'd mind if I waited for you up here, sir."

He holstered his gun. "Call me Custis. I mean to call her something even sillier the next time I see her. But, as we both seem to have survived, what can I do for you, Miss Flora?"

"My house is infested with army agents, including a horrid man they call Colonel Walthers. I think they expect my poor brother to return despite all the trouble he's in," she told him.

Longarm took off his hat and hung up his coat. "I know Walthers. You're right about him being horrid, but fair is fair, and your kid brother *did* run for home aboard a stolen horse after he'd given the army his home address. You'd be amazed how often deserters do that. I know I am. But nine out of ten young troopers who go over the hill head right for the home they put down on their enlistment papers. We just got word that your brother has been mean to the army some more. I can't say Walthers is a total fool if he means to wait and see where the kid runs to now. You still ain't told me why *you* ran *here*, Miss Flora."

She said, "I heard the soldiers talking about some army post up north they think Joseph just misbehaved on."

"We don't *think* it, ma'am. How many short gents in goat-hair chaps could be running about claiming to be Black Jack Slade in the flesh, even in the wildest West?"

She sighed and said, "I know. I hate to admit it, but that does sound like my poor sick brother. The soldiers said something about sending someone up there in the morning. I thought you might be heading that way, too."

58

He nodded. "I have to. It's my job. So, if you came to talk me out of it, I just can't oblige you, much as I'd like to."

"I know you have your job to do. But you're not like the others. You seem more gentle and understanding. I fear that should anyone *else* find Joseph first they may *hurt* him."

Longarm moved over to his dressing table to pour some Maryland rye into two tumblers, with a little pitcher water, as he told her, "No professional lawman worth his salt kills anyone he can bring in alive. Even if he's mean-natured, it looks better on his record if he brings prisoners in the hard way."

He held out a glass to her. "Sit down and drink this, even if you don't drink. We got to talk brass tacks."

She sat down with the tumbler but held it in her lap as she said, "I know Joseph is dangerous, but—"

"You don't know how dangerous he is," He cut in. "They don't allow girl children to go to war. You have to go through at least one war to know who's dangerous and who's just trying to stay alive." He took a swig of his own drink. "All right, there's no delicate way to put it. Them two men your brother shot it out with was veteran gunslingers, both armed, and on the prod to make an arrest, when your brother stepped into your parlor to discuss his disgust with military life with 'em."

"I know all that. I told you Joesph has an unpredictable temper, Custis."

He shook his head. "They should have predicted it. He was wanted for desertion and horse theft when he came in with a brace of sixguns strapped around his skinny hips. As I read the results, they was standing side by side not far from the door, and he was in the doorway or just inside when he slapped leather and *beat* them both. From the powder burns, he swung both guns up at once and fired both at once at point-blank range. It was still mighty fine shooting, considering one gun had to be in his left hand."

"Joseph is left-handed," she cut in. "We tried, and his teachers tried, to make him write right-handed but he had temper tantrums, and after a time everyone gave up."

He nodded. "For that I thank you. It goes in my notes and helps explain him a mite better. That still leaves him able to drill a man direct through the heart with either hand. That's what you get when you force a natural lefty to use his right hand more than he ever wanted to. We know he drew and fired without a word of warning or even that certain look lesser gunslicks get in their eyes as they're fixing to draw. Had those army agents had the merest hint they were up against anything more than what they took to be a mere kid, they'd at least have tried to do a thing about it in the short time they had left. But your brother didn't *give* them time. He moved faster than spit on a stove, and he had them dead or at least unconscious before they could have even guessed they were in trouble."

She tried a sip of the drink, winced, and asked, "What do you mean by dead or unconscious? Don't you mean they were killed instantly?"

He shook his head. "I told you I rode through a war. A heavy slug through the heart stops it instant. But, if it ain't too shocked as well, the brain can still work for a few seconds, and more than one man's been killed by a man he just killed. On the other hand, a .45 slug can knock one out with its shocking power, hitting almost anywhere in the trunk, if the victim is *relaxed* when he gets hit. Tensed up, the hydrostatic shock don't whip-snap through muscles near as much. So do you see the way it had to have happened, now?"

She swallowed and said, "I think so. You're suggesting those two men were standing there, relaxed and maybe talking in a soothing way to what they thought was a frightened boy, when—"

"I ain't *suggesting* it," he cut in. "It don't work no other way. So now we get to the ugly part. How in thunder can you expect any lawman to approach a natural disaster like your kid brother in a gentle, understanding way?"

"That's why you have to take me with you, Custis. *I* can talk to Joseph. He'd never draw his guns on *me*."

He raised an eyebrow as well as his glass, took a snort, and said, "You must have forgotten the bruised breastbone you showed me earlier, Miss Flora."

She insisted, "That's my point. He *hit* me. He didn't *shoot* me. Isn't it true the original Black Jack Slade was a wife beater, not a wife murderer?"

"It depends on which version you read. Some say they was sort of fond of one another and that she raised pure ned when the vigilantes come for him. I can see how, either way, gunning a gal could be against the code of such an otherwise surely cuss. But leave us not forget your kid brother ain't really the man he seems to think he is. Gals get killed all the time in penny dreadfuls. It's a matter of Wild West myth that Calamity Jane Canary was killed in a gunfight with Mormon Bill so's Deadwood Dick could avenge the death of his true love."

"That's silly. Everyone knows Calamity Jane was the sweetheart of Wild Bill Hickock," she said.

He smiled thinly. "That's a myth, too, even if old Jane likes it too much to deny it. I met James Butler Hickock when I first went to work for the Department. He was working mostly at getting drunk. He was also as happily married as a heavy drinker can get, to Agnes Lake, who was built a lot nicer than poor old Calamity, because she was a circus performer he'd met touring with a circus back East."

He took another slug and explained, "The point of all this tedious discussion is that even when things are down as public record in black and white, the gents who write the fairy tales your brother takes so serious don't allow a little thing like the truth to get in their way. Most of them can't even *know* the truth, writing as far off as London and stealing tall tales from one another. But your kid brother takes tall tales as his real world and, worse yet, he's fast enough to *back* his loco notions. I'd like to get my hands on the range instructor who taught him to handle guns so good. But they ain't sending me after *him*. It's your kid brother the law wants, and you can't come along to reason with anyone so unreasonable. I got enough on my plate with just *half* your family to worry about. I'd never forgive myself if you *both* wound up shot."

She raised the glass and downed the drink with a heroic effort before she put it on his lamp table and began to unbutton her bodice again. He put his own drink aside. "Just what do you think you're doing? I've already seen your bruises."

She smiled up at him sadly and said, "I can't go home, with those awful men tramping about my house. If you won't take me with you, couldn't I at least stay here with you tonight?"

She must have been able to read his thoughts, despite his valiant attempt at a poker face. For as she exposed her pretty little breasts to the lamplight she said, "It's not as if either of us are virgins, you know."

He said, "Speak for yourself. How pure I might or might not be is not the question. I ain't in position to compromise myself as an arresting officer."

She smiled up at him archly. "Heavens, what are you planning to arrest *me* for, Custis?" she asked.

He said, "Indecent exposure and cruelty to animals. It ain't going to work, Miss Flora. I admire your devotion to kin, but we both know what you're trying to do. You're just upsetting us both to no avail."

She gathered her duds together more sedately and started to cry. Her tears were real. He sat down beside her and buttoned her bodice back up as he said, "You can't stay here, for I know what any lawyer worth his salt could make of *that* in court. Pull yourself together and I'll take you over to a hackstand I know of in this neighborhood. It's too late and dark out to send a lady back across Cherry Creek on foot alone."

She didn't argue. She acted sort of numb until he had them both downstairs and walking quietly and awkwardly toward the lit-up corner where, with luck, he'd be able to find a ride home for her.

As he spotted an empty hack tethered in front of Mamma's Cantina he said, "There you go. I'll put you in and chase that fool driver out of that dive so's he can carry you home, or to a hotel if you'd rather. Do you need any money?"

She sobbed, grabbed hold of him, and buried her face against his chest as she cried, "Oh, I feel so cheap and low, now. Whatever must you think of me?"

He patted her back. It felt nice as he soothed, "I think you acted like a lady in desperation. The Lord gave you gals mighty unfair weapons. Had I thought you meant it, I might have taken you up on your cruel temptation. But it still wouldn't have stopped me from doing whatever I may have to do, later, and think how awful you'd feel if you gave your all to save your kid brother and we still wound up shooting it out."

"Isn't there any other way, Custis? I know Joseph is a killer, but he's sick. It's not really his fault!"

"I know that. He acted crazy the first time I laid eyes on him. I don't want to hurt him, Flora. I know that if I can bring him in alive they'll send him to the asylum, not the gallows or even prison. I know that if I fail, and live through it, you'll never forgive me. But that's the way it has to be."

He knew, later, as he watched her drive away, that his mind had done the right thing, no matter how mad the rest of him was sure to feel before he ever got to sleep in a lonesome room still haunted by her faint perfume.

Chapter 6

The U.P. Combination rolled into Julesburg late in the morning and stopped just long enough to let Longarm and his possibles off before rolling on to more important places. In its day Julesburg had rated a population close to two thousand, and a killing a day. But since the rails had replaced the Overland stages and freight wagons the population had dropped considerably. The town had become a sleepy little county seat and railroad juncture, where the wildest visitors were train-weary passengers changing trains, or cowhands off the surrounding spreads who only got drunk enough to be dangerous once a month, on payday. The town was a good ten miles or more west of the newly opened Ogallala cattle trail and so was seldom shot up by the rougher hands one tended to find on a long market drive.

Longarm picked up his McClellan saddle, with everything he'd brought along lashed to it, and crossed the dusty street to the weathered frame hotel across from the depot. The sleepy blonde behind the desk in the tiny lobby perked up when she saw such a rare sight as a possible guest on such an otherwise dull occasion. When he asked her if it was at all possible to hire a room she told him he could have his pick. He said he'd like a corner room at the east end of the top floor and she said he could have one and that she could see he was an experienced traveler on the summer prairie.

She sold him a key and came around from her side of the stand-up desk to carry his luggage, saying they'd had a bellhop, once, but that he'd run off to herd cows since the price of beef had risen. Longarm told her he hardly ever let ladies carry things for him but she went up the stairs ahead of him, anyway. He found the way she climbed the stairs with her tailbone moving almost as much as her feet an interesting novelty. It was too bad her face was no longer youthful, and that he wouldn't be staying long in any case.

She led him to the corner room. As he deposited his saddle over the foot of the double brass bedstead, she busied herself opening both windows, saying, "It'll smell better in here once the cross-venting airs it out some. We keep the windows closed when the rooms are empty to cut down on the dusting. That smell you may have noticed ain't what you might think. We don't have bugs. The handy man just oiled the bedsprings and, for some fool reason, he used bug oil instead of the axle grease I told him to use."

He said he could see they kept the place wholesome and asked her how many other hotels there might be in town. She looked hurt and said, "This is the best one and about the *only* one as takes in transients, anyways. You got to hire room and board by the week at the other places and none of 'em are any nicer than this."

He said he was sure of that. "The reason I'm asking is that, as I told you downstairs, I'm law. You'd remember, I hope, hiring a bed to a sort of wild-eyed little gent prone to Texas hats and goat-skin chaps?"

She nodded, but said, "We never. I know who you mean. The local law and the army police have already pestered me about that crazy cowboy as shot up the canteen out at the post. I told them, and so now I can tell you, that we ain't had a male guest of any description for a good three days, now. There was nobody here within twenty-four hours of the shoot-up but a secretary gal and a lady coming back from Denver with her sick little boy. She's had him in the lung spa there in hopes of a cure for his consumption."

Longarm raised an eyebrow. "Just how big a boy might we be talking about?"

She said, "Oh, six or eight, poor little thing. I doubt he'll ever see ten, for when we cleaned up after they caught their eastbound train there was blood on his pillowcase. Why do you ask? Do you know anyone like that?"

"Not that young. It was a grasp at a straw in any case. The little rascal I'm after don't act sane enough to have anyone but another lunatic as a confederate."

He dug out a dime to tip her, and though she said she was the owner and not a bellhop, she put it away anyhow and asked if he had any other possible desires. She looked disappointed when he told her, "Yep, I have to get out to Fort Halleck, now, and as I recall, it's a short ride but a long walk. So where would I find me a good livery stable here in town?"

She said there was one just a dozen doors east but then she said, "You'll have a time hiring a mount right now. Most of the able-bodied men and half the tough boys in town are out looking to cut the trail of that outlaw in the Texas hat. Since few keep horses regular, they'll have hired all the livery nags."

He shot a thoughtful glance at his saddle, shrugged, and said, "I'll leave my gear here and give her a try, anyway. I reckon I could leg it that far if I have to. But I'd feel dumb if I did so only to find out, later, that I didn't have to."

She followed him out and made no surly comments as he locked the door, pocketed the key, and wedged a match stem in the jamb. But as she led the way downstairs she told him, over her shoulder, "I ain't seen nobody use that trick since Black Jack Slade got run out of town."

He smiled thinly. "I didn't know my notion was that old. No offense, but you could hardly be old enough to remember the one and original Black Jack Slade, ma'am."

She dimpled at his gallant lie. "Call me Myrtle. I has to admit I was only a girl-child when my late husband brung me out here just afore the War. *He* worked for Overland, too. In them days everyone in town did, save for the tinhorns and the pimps trying to take advantage of the more honest folk traveling the trail. I know they say mean things about Black Jack. In fact, he could get a mite surly when he was in his cups. But he did keep the riffraff in their place whilst he was supervisor here."

Longarm didn't feel up to an argument on such a hot, dry day. He said, "I did hear tell he run the coach line honest, at least when he was sober, Myrtle."

"Black Jack took his job serious, drunk or sober. It was that French Canuck, Jules Beńe, who was crooking the company. My late husband told me so, and he was in a position to know, because he worked on the books in the office, here."

"Jules Bené would be the Jules they named the stage stop after, right?"

"As a matter of fact, he named Julesburg after his grasping self. There was nothing here but grass when they laid out the Overland Trail, and Jules Bené was the first supervisor. Bené prospered so good, so fast, that Mr. Ficklin in Council Bluffs, the firm's general manager, sent Black Jack Slade out here to look into the matter. It didn't take Jack long to see how sticky-fingered Bené was. Jack hired back some honest men Bené had fired for asking questions, and began to question them himself. It was right down the street Bené shot Black Jack in the back, twice, and pumped him full of number-nine buck as he lay there helpless. I didn't see the fight, but I heard the shots, and it was me as cradled what I took to be a dying man's head in my apron as Frenchy Bené laughed, said to bury him and send the bill to him, before he strutted off bold as brass."

"There was no law about to object to such rude behavior?"

She turned at the bottom of the stairs to grin up at him like the wicked child he suspected she must have been in her day. "Oh, the boys were going to string Bené up. My husband was the one as got the rope. But then Ben Ficklin in the flesh came. He'd read Black Jack's first reports and had meant to fire Frenchy Bené in any case. The company owned the town. Mr. Ficklin bossed the company. So when he said he didn't want a lynching on company property, the boys had to listen. Mr. Ficklin told Frenchy Bené to ride fast and hope he'd ridden far enough by the time Black Jack died. So Bené rode, and that was that. I don't mean to boast, but I was one of the ladies as nursed poor Black Jack back to health, and it wasn't easy. Nobody but a giant of a man could have soaked up so much lead and lived."

"Then I take it the original Black Jack was not what one could call a runt?"

She replied, sort of wistfully, "He was tall, dark, and handsome. Almost as big as you, but a lot more dark. That's why they called him Black Jack. He could have passed for a Sioux, and some said he had Injun blood. Didn't you know that?"

He said he hadn't thought about it, since the lunatic

who was trying to be Black Jack nowadays was short, pale, and puny. Then he ticked his hatbrim to her and headed for the doorway. As the sun outside slapped him in the face with a hot towel, the middle-aged Myrtle called after him, "Come back here if you can't hire even a mule. I might be able to fix you up."

When he got to the livery he discovered that she'd been right about the townees playing posse. The fat old stablehand there told him the only transportation they had left for hire was a pony cart. When Longarm asked if it would be at all possible to hire just the pony, the older man laughed and told him, "Anything's possible, but a man your size would sure look stupid aboard a Shetland mare. On the other hand, since you'd have both feet on the ground, you could likely get her to move a mite faster. Lord knows she'd need a little help in packing anyone your size. We mostly hire her out to women and children, cart and all."

Longarm almost let that go by him. Then he asked, "By the grasp of a straw, could you have hired that pony cart to a gent short enough to pass for a kid, say yesterday afternoon?"

The stablehand shook his head. "Nope. The sheriff was ahead of you on that. The cart was out exactly twice yesterday. A grandmother I've dealt with before took her grandkids from back East for a morning ride on the prairie. Later in the day, a young gal hired the rig to ride off alone in. I suspect she aimed to meet her fellow outside of town. She got back after sundown, looking sort of rolled in the grass, if you know what I mean. There was mud on the spokes. They likely did their spooning over in the willows along the South Platte."

Longarm frowned and said, "This is likely another wild guess, but Fort Halleck is along the South Platte. So can we be sure such a mysterious traveler was a woman, and not a short gent dressed silly as hell?"

The older man laughed knowingly. "She was pure

70

she, and built sort of tempting. I helped her out of the cart, and you know how a helping hand might grasp the situation sort of accidental. When I told the sheriff that he said I was a dirty old man. He should talk. Everyone in town except his wife knows about the sheriff and that young schoolmarm."

Longarm hadn't come all this way to listen to small-town gossip. "If your sheriff was so interested in that same young gal in that same pony cart, he must have had a reason. Did he say what it was?" he asked.

"Sure he did. He wanted to know if I'd hired any stock to anybody new in town, and when I told him I had, we got down to possibles. He said he figured some married man was carrying on over in the willows, too. The rascal who shot up Fort Halleck must have got out there on his own mount. There ain't a horse owned by anyone around here that can't be accounted for at the time of the shoot-up."

Longarm thanked him and headed back to his hotel, mulling over what he had been told. Assuming young Slade had been keeping that purloined army mount somewhere in Denver and had started riding just after he sung so awful in the Parthenon, it still wouldn't work. Following the South Platte and its forage and water all this way would have taken even a horse-killer more than the time they had to work with. Aside from having to ride faster than the Pony Express ever had, and then some, the country between here and Denver, while still mighty open, wasn't so open that a stranger of any description going lickety-split on a lathered horse would not get noticed at all.

By the time he got back all the way he had decided his want had gotten to Julesburg the way he had, by train. There was just no way to ride a horse, invisible, for a good hundred and fifty miles in less than three days, even if one hated his horse. Just as important, the rascal had ridden off, on something, after shooting up that army canteen. So unless he'd boarded a late-night train paying half-fare for a four-legged kid under twelve, which hardly seemed likely, he'd found a mount at this end of the trip.

Longarm went over that gal in the pony cart again. They had not reported a gal shooting up Fort Halleck. On the other hand, a gal could change into a cow outfit and likely pass for at least a short cowhand. But that raised more questions than it answered. The army could hardly have mistaken even a skinny little recruit for a gal, casual as some medical exams might be. While the sly old dog at the livery could hardly have mistaken a he for a she as he stole a feel. Black Jack Junior had to be a he. If he didn't want folk to know where he was or what he was up to, he'd only have to calm down. Nobody noticed a mousy little runt who behaved halfway sensibly.

Myrtle greeted Longarm in the lobby and asked how he'd made out. He said, "They didn't have a single horse for sale or hire."

"Well, I won't sell you my Blue Boy, but you can ride him all you like for two bits a day," she said.

He brightened and said he hadn't known she kept her own stock.

"I was hoping you'd be able to pick one up at the livery," she said. "I don't like to hire out my personal mount. Blue Boy has a tender mouth and he's used to carrying considerably less weight. But if you promise to ride him gentle, and look out for prairie-dog holes, I'll hire him out just this once."

He agreed to treat her Blue Boy like a brother and ran up to get his own gear as she called after him that she'd meet him out back. In his room he shucked his coat and string tie. It was going to get hotter before it got cooler. He lugged his gear downstairs and, sure enough, found Myrtle talking to an old steel-gray gelding in the stable out back. She was feeding the brute dining-room sugar cubes and telling it not to be afraid as Longarm joined them to observe mildly, "It's your horse, ma'am. But they like apples or even carrots just as well, and such treats don't rot their teeth as bad."

She said she knew Blue Boy was spoiled, but that she'd never been able to resist a pleading male. He was too polite to point out that a gelding wasn't exactly a male, once it had been cut. He told the sleek critter how much he liked it, too, and had no trouble saddling up. Getting Blue Boy's sweet teeth to accept the bit he'd brought along as well was more trouble. Myrtle said he was used to her own bridle and he agreed, grudgingly, since while it was in fact a bridle, it was silver-mounted sissy, and the bit was intended more for spoiling pets than serious riding. As he led the spoiled pet out into the alley, Myrtle followed, and as he mounted up she warned him not to lope too fast in the cruel, hot sun.

He assured her he'd keep to the shady side of the trail and as he heeled Blue Boy into motion—*slow* motion—it became obvious that, whatever they might be up to, even a brisk trot could not be what the lazy critter had in mind.

He waited until they'd strolled out of sight before he kicked harder and growled, "I know it's almost noon and that there ain't no shady side of the Overland Trail. But the sooner we get out of this sun the better, so *move* you otherwise total waste of sugar cubes!"

Blue Boy stopped dead in his tracks, turned his head back to roll one reproachful eye at Longarm, but decided not to bite his boot tip after all when Longarm stared back sternly and said, "Go on. Just you try it and I'll kick your sugar-rotted teeth up into your empty skull."

Blue Boy had some brains, after all. He heaved a defeated sigh and commenced to trot. That jarred a rider astride more than it might a lady seated side-saddle, but it was a mile-eating if uncomfortable pace, and it was,

73

in fact, too hot at this hour to lope a critter he'd promised to return in good shape.

As they trotted the trail, raising enough dust for a Cheyenne war party, Longarm noted other drifting dust above the horizon all around. That meant the posse riders had split up to circle wide for sign on the flatter prairie this far east of the front ranges. Longarm doubted they'd cut much sign as he stared at the overgrazed range closer to the trail. The 'dobe soil was summer baked as hard as the bricks one could make from it, without having to fire. At this time of the year you could maybe cut it with a knife, but even a steel-shod hoof wouldn't leave a serious mark on it. The scrubbrush stubble of wiry dry shortgrass would no more hold a hoofprint than a welcome mat on a brick porch. He glanced to the south, where the South Platte had to be running, if there was water in it. For water was the thing to consider when tracking Cheyenne or worse out here in high summer. But he saw by more rising dust that the others looking for Black Jack Junior had that bet covered. If he'd watered his mount over that way it would soon be known. So there was no need for side tripping, and the sooner he got to the army post the sooner they'd be able to fill in some missing facts for him.

It might not have taken that long by the clock but it felt like they'd been trotting on a hot stove all day by the time they got to Fort Halleck.

The name was sort of boastful. The army outpost had never been what one thought of as a fort, back when it had been built to keep an eye on wild buffalo and rampaging Indians pestering the Overland Trail. Since then both the buffalo and the Indians had been whittled down considerably, and there was only a modest post-operating company of army engineers stationed there.

As he turned off the trail running past it, Longarm

saw they had nobody posted at the main gate, which was more like a gap in the three-strand bobwire around the quarter section or so. A sun-faded flag hung listlessly from a lodgepole flagstaff that sure could have used more whitewash. The buildings on the far side of the dust-paved parade could have started out most any color. Twenty-odd years of summer dust and winter snow had turned them all to what looked sort of like big gray pasteboard shoe boxes.

He spied a sign that had once been gold and red in front of post headquarters and reined in to dismount. As he was tethering Blue Boy near a watering trough nobody had thought to put water in of late, a burly sergeant came out on the veranda

"This is U.S. Army property, cowboy. Are you authorized to be on this post?" he asked.

Longarm moved up to join him in the shade. "If I wasn't, I'd be here anyway, thanks to all the guards you have along your wispy fence. But don't get your bowels in an uproar, Sarge. I am federal, too. Deputy U.S. Marshal Custis Long. I'm here to look into that shoot-up you had out here last evening."

The sergeant said, "Oh, you'd best talk to the commander, then," and led him inside to talk to an overage-in-grade first lieutenant. Longarm had to take their word about his rank. The poor red-faced cuss was sitting at his desk in his undershirt with a bottle of sloe gin, half empty, in front of him. He stared up morosely at Longarm. "They wired us some army investigators was on their way to look into the incident. We're under orders not to discuss army business with anyone else," he told Longarm.

Longarm said, "I know Colonel Walthers of old. We can work this out two ways. You can let me poke about and talk to any of your men who might have witnessed what went on or you can order me off your post, in writing, signed, so I can offer that as evidence that you refused the help of the Justice Department when it was offered."

The lieutenant looked even sadder. "I don't think I want to do that. I was taught my first day in the army to never be first, never be last, and never volunteer. I don't want trouble with any federal department. Why don't you just leave quiet?"

Longarm said, "I'll be glad to, if you order me off your post in writing. I don't like to be in trouble neither, and my boss is twice as mean as any colonel. He told me to come up here and investigate the shoot-up on this post. Your move."

The burly sergeant snarled, "You heard what the lieutenant said," and grabbed Longarm's arm to haul him outside. Longarm planted a left cross in his face, sending him to the floor. He whipped out his .44-40 and told the man rising on the far side of the desk, "That was not a good move. I know I can't lick a whole company of engineers, but I got five in this wheel and two more in my belly derringer. You ain't getting me to leave, alive, without a note to the teacher. So what's it going to be?"

The lieutenant sank back down, helped himself to an unhealthy belt of gin, and said, "Damn it, you heard me say I didn't want any trouble. Go over to the canteen and talk to the corporal in charge, if you must. But you'd better leave before Sergeant Fagan, there, wakes up again."

"Don't you have any control over him, Lieutenant?"

"I don't know. He's the bully of the post, and nobody's ever knocked him out before."

Longarm holstered his gun and left. He led Blue Boy to the long, and low building with "Post Canteen" painted above its door and tethered his mount on the shady side. He went in and found at least a full platoon lounging about at the camp tables scattered across the sawdusted floor. He bellied up to the smaller than usual bar and told the corporal behind it he wanted a beer and a rundown on the visit of Black Jack Junior, in that order.

The beer was the watery stuff the army allowed on post and the enlisted barkeep said he hadn't been there, adding, "Grogan, the regular man, here, never knew what hit him. I'm his replacement."

Longarm turned to brace his elbows on the bar as he asked if anyone there had seen the fight. A tall, skinny private who looked too old to be in the army said, "I was sitting right about here. I wound up in yon corner before the smoke cleared. The son of a bitching civilian kilt the man I was talking to, and two others, before he shot out the lamp and left, yelling like a banshee. Two others was hit, but not as serious."

Longarm glanced up to see that the shiny brass lamp now hanging from the low rafters was the only thing in the place that looked new. "Did anybody hear what the fuss was about?"

Another, more intelligent-looking soldier said, "Not every word. But as the conversation was short and sharp I suspect I can put it together fair enough. This sawed-off cowboy strode in like he owned the place and demanded a drink. Since this is a pure army canteen it's safe to assume old Grogan told him he couldn't serve civilians here. Then Grogan was dead and all hell was busting loose. The cute little rascal had two big .45s and they sure did echo under that low ceiling. I ain't sure Slim's right about him leaving with a banshee wail. It sounded more like singing to me."

"It was," another man said, "I heard it. It was that mean song the cavalry sings about us engineers. The one that goes, 'The Engineers has dirty ears, the dirty sons of bitches.'"

There was a murmur of agreement. Longarm nodded. "I can see why the post regulations against serving civilians is not in force right now. You say two of the men he shot was only wounded?"

The barkeep behind him said, "That was after he shot out the lamp. Grogan went down right where I'm standing, with his shirt on fire and his heart blown out his back. Murphy, standing about where you are now, took one through the heart as well. The other two was hit more casual but just as dead."

Longarm left his own gun holstered but raised his hand to aim at the new lamp with his index finger. "Yeah, the rascal is better, point blank. That couldn't have been much comfort to the boys he had to aim at. I suspect I know, but could any of you give me a good description of the killer?"

The one called Slim said, "Who could forget him? He was knee-high to a grasshopper, had on a big black hat meant for a bigger skull, and I remember wondering why on earth anyone would want to wear fur chaps in open country in such hot weather."

"Goat-skin chaps, black and white?" asked Longarm.

"They was black and white and hairy," Slim said. "I never got to ask him whether he'd skint a goat or not. Oh, he had on big Mex spurs. The kind that jingle."

"Over high heels or low?"

"High and Texas, as I recall. It didn't make him all that tall, though, now that I picture him some more."

Another man offered, "I have a kid brother back home about the same size. He's twelve. The one as shot all them boys looks a bit older, but not much. I'd say you was looking for a crazy young cowboy about fourteen or sixteen."

Longarm knew Black Jack Junior was in his twenties, but the description fit the mean little cuss he'd had words with in the Parthenon, and two such critters running loose made no sense at all. So he finished his weak beer, thanked them one and all for their help, and went back outside.

As he was untethering Blue Boy, the burly Sergeant Fagan came around the corner, eyes glaring as well as swelling shut, by now. Longarm nodded pleasantly and said, "Howdy. I'm sorry I had to do that, Sarge. But don't never lay hands on a grown man unless you mean it."

"The lieutenant just gave me a direct order not to do that no more while you're on this post. Is it safe to assume you mean to stay in Julesburg long?" the bully asked.

"No longer than I have to. But I may be there the next time you're off duty," Longarm said.

Fagan said, "I'm glad. For the next time we meet I'll be in my civvies, wearing my sidearm. Consider yourself warned."

Longarm said, "Thanks, I'll keep your word of cheer in mind. I hope you know you're talking dumb, though. I'm packing a badge as well as a gun. The gun is double-action. So I'd be taking unfair advantage of you, even if you got lucky."

"Are you afraid to face a man, fair, after coldcocking him?"

"Sure I am. You're a lot bigger than the gunslick they sent me after, and you're talking almost as wild. I didn't cold-cock you. You laid hands on me first and, like I said, getting hit goes with the poorly studied move. I don't care if you're still sore about that. But I want you to listen to my own friendly word of warning. If you make me hurt you more serious, I'll no doubt be let off. I've met idjets like you before and, as you can see, they ain't hung me yet. If you take me, and I doubt you can, they'll hang you for murder and we'll *both* be dead."

"See here! A man has rights, and you just busted my nose."

"I said I was sorry, and *you'd* best see here as well. Things ain't the way they might have been in the bad old days, and even Black Jack Slade got swung when

79

things might have seemed more casual out here. So you'd best simmer down. I know more than one lawman, less kind-hearted than me, who'd just love to add you to his rep. Fortunately for you, I ain't looking for a rep. But if you ever meet my sidekicks, Smiley and Dutch, from the same Denver office, watch your fool mouth. They've often chided me for my more gentle manners."

As he swung into his saddle, Fagan bawled, "I ain't afraid of any damn civilian. In my day I've fought Sioux and worse!"

Longarm didn't answer that he'd seen his share of Indian fighting. There was no sense wasting words on a pure fool. He could only hope the fool was only sounding off. He hated it when men told him in advance they were gunning for him. He never knew, when next they met, whether to say howdy or go for his gun.

Chapter 7

Having given fair warning before noon, the prairie sun was doing its best to kill everything in sight as it glared down from its inverted bowl of cloudless cobalt sky.

They were a little more than halfway back to town when Longarm spied dust rising from the trail ahead and told Blue Boy, "Easy, now. That ain't a whirlwind coming at us. Some other damn fool is on the trail in this infernal heat."

Blue Boy cocked his ears and broke into a happy lope toward what Longarm could now see was a pony cart coming to meet them. It had to be the one the livery hired out for women and children to ride in. It took him only a mite longer to see that the woman abusing the pony in front of her was Myrtle from the hotel. She was wearing the same polka-dot dress, but at least she'd had the sense to shade her head with a big straw picture hat.

As they met, Blue Boy sniffed at her like a begging pup and, sure enough, she fed him another sugar cube and patted his muzzle. She told Longarm, "I was getting worried about you two. All the other riders from town have been back a spell, and thermometers are starting to bust in the shade."

Longarm told her risking a sunstroke herself was no way to make it any cooler. "I watered this critter just before we left the post, and he spent most of the time out there in the shade. I wish I'd been made to feel as welcome. You say the posse riders have given up on Black Jack Junior?" he asked.

She said, "They had to. He's long gone, wherever he went. The two riders who work for me—as hotel help, not riders—just told me they'd checked with all the surrounding spreads and homesteads for miles, and that nobody's seen hide nor hair of the mean little thing. As soon as I had someone to watch the desk I came after you to make sure you hadn't killed my Blue Boy and to tell you you can stop looking."

"I wish I could. But my boss has his mind set. The kid ain't anywhere around here, though. So what say we head for the nearest shade?"

He had meant Julesburg, of course, but she shot him an arch look from the shade of her hatbrim. "That would be a place I know, over by the river. We could enjoy a nice swim and, with something like that in mind, it just so happens I packed a picnic hamper to bring along."

He looked dubiously down at her. "Miss Myrtle, that same South Platte runs through Denver, a lot closer to the hills, and even *there,* it ain't deep enough to swim in at this time of the year."

"A lot you know. Follow me and I'll show you a spot where a gravel operation left the river deep enough to drown in."

Without waiting for an answer, she swung her pony around and drove off the trail. He followed her south, dubiously. Billy Vail hadn't sent him all this way to go swimming with women. On the other hand, heat-stroke

82

had to be above and beyond the call of duty, and Black Jack Junior was as likely to be in the South Platte as anywhere else in the county right now.

It only took them a few minutes, and as they smelled the water, both Blue Boy and the cart pony got harder to handle. They busted through the wall of crack-willow and taller cottonwood rising like a planted hedgerow along the uncertain banks of the wide but shallow stream and let both animals drink like camels, standing fetlock-deep in the tea-warm running water.

As Longarm took in the pleasant view he saw that this stretch of the South Platte was a lot wider than the same stream that ran through Denver. To make up for that, with less water this far from the mountain creeks that fed the South Platte, the misnamed river had become a glorified Cherry Creek, with the water braided between flat islands covered with sedge, brush, and even small trees. It was hard for a tree to grow up all the way on an island that got shifted about as the water level tried to make up its mind whether it was a summer trickle or a spring flood.

Myrtle said, "Let's go. The swimming hole I told you about is out beyond that willow bar."

He figured she should know. So he didn't argue as they moved on across the running water. It wasn't much deeper than Cherry Creek, but it was a lot wider, and he had to hope that kid story about quicksand was just a kid story. The wheels of the pony cart ahead sank in sort of ominously here and there. But then they were on the willow bar and the terra was not only firma but covered with lush green grass between the twisted tree trunks. As he dismounted and they tethered the critters on long leads to nibble, he already felt a lot cooler in the dappled shade. He said so, and told her she was smart to know of such an eden in a land that was mostly hell. She dimpled and told him, "Our swimming hole is yonder, through the trees. I mean to swim in my shimmy shirt, of course. I hope you're wearing under-drawers as well."

He assured her he had to, under tweed pants, if he wanted to ride at all. So she took a checked cloth from the cart, spread it on the grass, and placed her picnic hamper on it before she calmly tossed her hat aside and proceeded to shuck her dress.

Longarm had to gulp as he viewed the results. Her thin cotton chemise was so short it left little to the imagination. And for a gal who was no longer young, Myrtle had a body few teenagers could have matched. The same hard life that had hardened her features had kept her slim body and shapely limbs firm and limber. Without waiting for him, she laughed like a kid and ran across the grass to dive headfirst into what looked as shallow as the stretch they'd just forded. But she dove deep, stayed under a few strokes, and came up laughing, with her blond hair plastered to her skull and hanging down with a lot more shine and color now.

He wondered what he was doing with his duds still on and made haste to shuck and join her, naked save for his summer longjohns of somewhat more substantial cotton. The water felt just right as he dove into it. The long trip across the summer prairie had taken all the mountain sting out of it. It was just too warm to drink and a hell of a lot cooler than the air. He opened his eyes below the surface to see that, sure enough, the bottom he was gliding across was mossy gravel, and that Myrtle was blond all over. She was standing on the bottom with her chemise fluttering with the current above her waist and even her belly button was cute as hell.

He surfaced beside her to take his mind off such matters, splashed her, and swam about some more to explore the limits of the gravel pit and get his mind on something—*anything*—but the way that sassy chemise of hers refused to stay where it was supposed to. She swam some, but not as much, and it seemed that no matter where he swam in the modest-sized leeway he kept seeing her bare behind or exposed front ahead of him. He was suffering a raging erection when she called out, "I'm cooled off enough to eat, now. How about you?"

As they climbed out he could only hope he was bent over enough to keep from giving her the notion he wasn't really thinking about food.

But once they were stretched out side by side on the checked ground cloth, enjoying the sandwiches she'd made, as they let the warm shade dry their bare skin and soggy underwear, he was surprised at his own appetite. He'd forgotten until just now that he'd not eaten since morning, and it had to be midafternoon by now. The butter she'd spread on the wheat bread had melted and soaked in. The cold meat she'd placed between slices tasted cooked and the iced tea she'd brought to wash the eats down with tasted fresh from the pot after soaking up all that sun on the trail. But he said he couldn't recall a grander picnic spread, and he meant it.

She thanked him and looked sort of wistful as she added, "I guess a widow woman with nothing better to offer has to work more than most on her cooking, huh?"

He smiled reassuringly at her. "Don't mean-mouth yourself, ma'am. You can't be any older than me and you don't hear *me* bemoaning my lost youth, do you?"

"You're joshing but I love it, you sweet child. We both know I was a woman grown and married before the War."

"Well, that was only about fifteen years ago, and I was in the War, too. I disremember which side I rode for. We was all young and foolish, once."

"You must have been a baby if *you* were in the War. They should have been ashamed of themselves for letting anyone so young join up."

He shrugged a bare shoulder. "I thought they was

85

sort of taking advantage of me, too, before it was over. My point is that even if you was old enough to go to war that long ago, you can't have more than a couple of years on me."

She sighed and said, "More like ten. Don't you think I look in the mirror when I pin up my hair? It's just not *fair*. It hardly seems yesteryear since I was young and pretty."

"Oh, hell, you ain't that bad. I'm more tanned and beat-up than you are and you don't hear me crying about it, do you?"

She said, "It's different for you men. Time doesn't treat a man as cruel as it does a woman."

"You're wrong, no offense. Time treats us all about the same, and it's human notions that's cruel. You poor gals is supposed to look like teenagers forever, whilst us brutes just get mature or, if we've really been beat-up, distinguished. A gent can sport a saber scar and gray sideburns and still be considered good-looking. You poor little things ain't allowed to have one laugh wrinkle if you still want men to admire you and women to hate you."

She sighed. "Do you think you have to tell any girl over thirty that? If I was a man, right now, they'd say I was just in my prime instead of an aging innkeeper. But I must say you're awfully understanding, Custis. How come you understand us women so well?"

He said, "Some of my best friends is women. Maybe I talk to them more than some gents. That ain't saying I *understand* them. All any man can do is try."

She favored him with a sort of motherly smile. "You do, don't you, you sweet boy." Then she laughed, perhaps at herself, and said, "I'll bet you don't go swimming with many as old as me, though."

He looked sincerely blank. "Hell, I've kissed gals older than you in my time."

She answered, "Oh?" and moved the hamper from between them to lie back and murmur, with her eyes closed, "Prove it!"

He did. It didn't hurt and, from the way she responded to his almost brotherly attempt at reassurance, she liked it even better.

He wasn't sure he ought to go farther. His life was already complicated enough and he felt sure the gal wanted to feel pretty again. So he kept his hands polite as she wrapped her bare arms around him and pulled him down half atop her. He knew he'd been right about how young and firm her breasts looked as he felt them pressed wetly to his naked chest. He decided it was time to stop while they were both ahead. But as he came up for air she moaned, "Oh, you will be gentle, won't you? It's been so long and you seem so big and strong."

He saw he was in trouble, now, no matter how he answered that. So, choosing the lesser of two evils, he assured her he would and though he meant it, she wouldn't *let* him do it gentle, once they got started. She had a lovely body, too, as she moved it up and down with both skill and enthusiasm, with little pinpoints of sunlight dappling her firm smooth naked flesh. She beat him to a protracted climax. As he stopped and just lay there enjoying a warm soak she ran her palms over him from nape to buttocks, like a little girl surprised by Santa on a Christmas morning she hadn't been expecting, and crooned, "Oh, thank you. I'd forgotten how good that really felt, even though I've been dying for it for a long, long time."

He kissed her and said, "It ain't over yet. Just let me get my breath back."

Later, they went swimming again to cool off, and she was even more fun to swim with bare-ass entire, since they found a mighty interesting position that just wouldn't have worked on dry land. But by the time they were back on the grass, though she was more than willing to try yet another athletic way, he sensed they were starting to show off more than they were still enjoying it. So, as they rested in each others's arms and shared a smoke, he suggested, "It's getting late, and the old livery man is sure to gossip if I get you back to town after sundown. He does about other gals who meet gents out on the prairie in that pony cart."

She snuggled closer. "Pooh, I don't care." Then she sat up on one elbow to peer down at him uncertainly. "I guess *you* do? It's one thing to take pity on an old lady out here where nobody can laugh at you, but another thing entire to be seen on the streets of Julesburg with her."

He had not, as a matter of fact, meant to boast of his conquest back in town. But Longarm had been raised to believe in simple justice, as many an outlaw had been forced to notice. So he said, "I am forced by my job to move on a lot, just as I'm getting fond of a sweet little thing like you. But if you want to go steady as long as I'll be around Julesburg, it's jake with me, public or private. It's your reputation, not mine."

"Oh, you darling man!" But then, being a woman and thinking the same way, she said, "We'd better be discreet. It is a small, spiteful town. If you really still want me, I can sneak up to your room easy enough, late at night when all the gossips are asleep. But I don't think we ought to act too familiar in front of folk, do you?"

"It could cause talk. But what in thunder are we arguing about? I just told you I didn't give a hang one way or the other."

She said, "I know. If I asked you to take me to dinner at the depot diner, in front of God and everybody, would you?"

He said, "Sure. Why not?"

And she began to cry as she told him, "Oh, we couldn't! I'd *never* live it down. But you've no idea how nice and naughty and *young* you've made me feel by *offering*."

Chapter 8

They got back to Julesburg before sundown. Since she seemed more worried than he did about their wild fling, Longarm suggested they enter town separately and assured her he'd meet her later at the hotel, whether he'd have time to kiss her some more or not. She asked what he meant, and he explained that he meant to check the telegraph office in case the man he was after had turned up somewhere else. She looked so hurt that he promised, "I have to check out even if I have to leave, don't I? I can't wait to try those freshly oiled bedsprings, can you?"

She blushed and drove on ahead of him as he lit another smoke to give her a lead the village biddies might find acceptable.

As he rode in alone, he saw he had the main street all to himself. Despite the low sun and lengthening shadows it was still hot enough to bake potatoes in the road dust.

He rode Blue Boy around to the back of the hotel,

unsaddled and rubbed him down, and left him in the stall, where Myrtle had already left more oats and water than the brute deserved.

He walked down the alley to a gap between the buildings and came out to the sleepy center of things to look about for a Western Union sign. He spotted one about where it should have been, near the depot, and strode over to it.

As he approached, two gents who'd been sitting and whittling in the shade of the office awning rose to greet him. Longarm sighed and said, "Aw, hell, why would even Billy Vail want to do a dumb thing like that?"

The two junior deputies from his home office were best known as Smiley and Dutch. The tall one, Smiley, was a morose, hatchet-faced breed who never smiled. It was his name. The shorter and stockier Dutch smiled all the time, even when he wasn't telling one of his endless dirty jokes. He was called Dutch because his German-American last name was so hard to pronounce they had all given up on it. Dutch didn't care. He said he only got sore when someone called him something dirty. He'd proven that more than once by slapping leather over something as mild as "bastard," and it was wildly held he would gutshoot a gent and drag him atop an ant pile to die slow for "son of a bitch."

As they shook, outside the Western Union, Smiley said, "There ain't no messages for you inside. We just asked. We figured you'd show up here sooner or later, though."

"Never mind how you hunted me down. Why in hell did they send you? I never asked for backup, no offense," Longarm said.

Dutch said, "Old Billy felt you might need some, anyway. Didn't you meet all them War Department assholes on the trail? We was told you'd headed out for Fort Halleck, and that was where *they* said they was headed, too."

Longarm said, "We must have missed each other as I was off the trail, heeding the call of nature. What about 'em? We already knew the army was after the same want."

Smiley said, "The boss sent us when he found out a short-colonel called Walthers was coming up here, personal, to pick a fight with you. We made the same train as it was pulling out and, since they didn't know who we was, we got to listen as they called you all sorts of mean names. Old Walthers kept saying he meant to arrest you, even though one of the gents with him kept saying he didn't see how they could. We got the distinct impression old Walthers wants *you* more than he wants that young cuss who keeps shooting soldier boys. So we stand ready to back you if he tries. What makes you so popular with that stuck-up pain in the ass, Longarm?"

Their superior officer shrugged. "I've been a pain in *his* ass, through no fault of my own. A while back we had a heated argument over another prisoner we both had papers on, and I won. Later, me and Billy, personally, kept Walthers from mowing down a mess of coal miners when we solved a case that turned out to be a plain old crime instead of the labor unrest the army gets to deal with so noisy at times. I don't know why Colonel Walthers takes things so personal, but he does."

Dutch laughed and said, "I know. I was in the army one time, too. There's a brand of army asshole that's so used to giving orders that it just goes loco when a man who don't *have* to obey army orders points that out and, knowing you, you tends to say things plainer than some. I've heard you talk back to Billy Vail in a manner that would drive even a sensible short-colonel to total madness."

Longarm chuckled. "As a matter of fact, I just this day drove a career sergeant sort of mad, and we was talking about you two today, too. I'm sorry I did, now. If either of you see a gent, wearing army blue or not, but sporting a nice set of shiners, keep an eye on his gun hand. His name is Fagan. I think he's just a windy bully. But he's dumb as hell, and if Walthers is out there cussing my name and allowing he'd like to see me dead or worse, there's no telling what a really stupid bastard nursing a grudge and a busted nose might think he could get away with."

Dutch laughed and said, "Let 'em come, all of 'em. I could never abide anyone above my rank when I was in the army, and for some reason I never got no higher than private."

"Our department ain't allowed to declare war on the War Department," Longarm told him. "I mean that. Colonel Walthers can rave all he wants, but he knows he can't do shit unless we give him an excuse. You go gunning any soldiers, even in self-defense, and you'll be filling out papers past Christmas. So pay no attention to the boys in blue. What's the latest on that boy in the goat-skin chaps?"

Smiley said, "There ain't none. Not since he shot up the army last night. Billy wired the sheriff's department, here. They wired back they couldn't pick up the rascal's trail and that, unlike the War Department, they'd take all the help they could get. They never said they'd back you against the army, though. That's what Billy sent *us* to do."

"Forget the fool army," Longarm said. "You couldn't have left the home office less than, say, four hours ago, so . . . Never mind. It was a dumb notion. It was more than four hours ago I heard the posse had given up and come on home. Let's go get a drink. If anything new has happened this afternoon, they'll have heard about it in the saloons."

As the three of them headed for the nearest set of swinging doors in sight, across the street, Smiley asked where Longarm had been all day if it hadn't been here or Fort Halleck.

Longarm said, "I was out over on the river, between here and there, scouting for sign."

"Find anything interesting?"

"Not sign. Save for the ground near the water, the whole wide prairie is so baked a man could drive a locomotive across it, off the tracks, and it wouldn't leave a trail to follow."

Smiley said, "Billy asked us to ask about trains *on* tracks as we was riding one. So we did. The conductor we talked to said he had a flier from both the War and Justice Departments, as well as his own timetable. So he'd been working on that angle, too. He said but one train passed through these parts after the time of that last shooting, and that the crew would surely have noticed if a cowboy in fancy chaps had ridden it anywhere with a horse."

Longarm waited until they passed through the saloon entrance and bellied to the bar before he said, "I read the same timetable, and our Black Jack Junior would have had to cut it fine even if the train crew was blind."

"He could have changed his duds," said Smiley.

Longarm signaled the barkeep over before he answered, "There was still no way he could have made it all the way back from Fort Halleck afoot before that Denver-bound combo stopped here just long enough to switch tracks and jerk water. I considered him getting about on foot, jingle-jangle spurs or not. It won't work. On the other hand, had he ridden back from that army post and caught a handy train out of town, he'd have had to leave the infernal *mount* some damned where, and there's been no reports on horses missing or turning up extra. We need three beers here, pard."

The barkeep filled three schooners as Dutch began to tell a joke about a saloon cat pissing in beer schooners. But Longarm told him, "I heard it, and it wasn't funny the first time. Get *serious*, damn it. I don't mind saying

I'm open to suggestions, because no matter how that loco kid done it, he done it, and the trail is a lot colder than this beer."

"Let's go on home, then," Smiley said. "There's no sense looking for a want where he ain't been seen for almost twenty-four hours, and the rascal has run back to Denver *before,* you know."

Longarm shook his head. "By now even he has to know we have his home address and, even if he don't, it's staked-out and he'd have walked into the trap by this time if that was his plan."

Dutch said, "Not if he's still riding that horse. He wouldn't be a third of the way there yet, even if he just shot up that canteen and headed right for home."

Longarm started to tell him how dumb that sounded. Then he said, "I'd best put that on the wire. It makes more sense than that dubious train. I know for a fact there's green grass and water all the way to Denver if you follow the river. You boys stay here and try to stay out of trouble for now."

He left them to warm suds and their own devices and legged it back to the Western Union. He picked up a yellow blank and a pencil that could have used some sharpening and wrote a message. He took it to the desk and told the night clerk, "I want this sent flat-rate to the sheriff's department of every county between here and Denver that the same river runs through, hear?"

The clerk read the message, whistled, and said, "I don't blame you. But we're talking about five counties at five cents a word, if you include this one."

Longarm said, "He might have stopped most any-where for a swim in such hot weather. But make that just Logan, Morgan, Weld, and Adams. He'd have been caught by now if he was still anywhere in this county, and I mean to have a word with your sheriff in any case, come morning."

The clerk said he'd get the intercept on the wire and

added, "You don't have to wait that long if you want to talk to our own county law, Deputy Long. I can't swear the sheriff in the flesh ain't gone home for supper by now, but the city hall stays open late in summer to make up for the noon siesta."

Longarm thanked him, asked for directions, and left. The frame city hall wasn't far, and sure enough all the windows were lit up.

Inside, a sweaty fat boy seated near the door told Longarm the sheriff had just stepped out, but that he'd be back. When he asked if there was anything they could do for him Longarm said, "Yeah, I'd like to talk to your county clerk, if he's still here."

The fat boy gave him the room number and added that, whether the boss was in or not, his secretary gal was, since he'd just fetched her some coffee.

Longarm moved down the musty corridor, wishing someone had had the sense to open a window, even though he couldn't see any window. He got to the office of the county clerk. It was a lot cooler inside, because the redhead seated at the desk *had* been smart enough to open the window behind her, and to hell with the miller moth that was fluttering around the hanging lamp above her. She wore specs and had a pencil stuck in the bun of her upswept carrot top. As she smiled up at him, he cursed himself for being so hasty in a strange town. She was downright lovely, and her bodice wasn't hiding as much of her shape as she might have thought.

She asked what she could do for him. He introduced himself, told her who he was after, and explained, "If the young lunatic we're after thinks he's old Black Jack Slade, it might help me to know more about his mentor. Penny dreadfuls just guess about a lot of things he done and, more important, run. I know it was before your time, ma'am. It was even before my time. But if you have any county records at all, written by folks as was there instead of guessing, back East or further . . ."

She jumped up and said, "As a matter of fact, I did notice some old county records about the famous gunslick, as I was filing something else a spell back. I hope I remember where I saw them."

He hoped so, too, and feared she might not, by the time she finally hauled a dusty folder from a drawer, blew on it as if that might help, and offered him the use of her desk to spread the folder open on. She said she was going to get some more coffee, asked if he'd like some, and when he took her up on it she said she'd be right back and left him alone with the one and original Black Jack Slade. She didn't fool him. He knew she was taking advantage of his interest as an excuse to get up and about for a spell.

There was a picture of the old-time killer. It looked not a thing like Slade had on that magazine cover. But then, had anyone back East thought to look at real pictures and records, they wouldn't put out such silly versions.

The picture was a woodcut. If it had been made freehand, the artist had likely been pretty bad. If it had been made from an old tintype, Black Jack had been sort of odd-looking. He was posed sideways, but one could see his eyes were glaring mean at someone off to the side. He looked about forty, with his black hair thinning at the temples but thick and wavy everywhere else. He had a big nose, thin tight lips, and a weak chin. He was smooth-shaven, but the woodcut artist had covered his whole face with fine lines as if to show he had some awful skin condition or more likely to show how dark his skin had been.

Longarm had already known that, and he never expected to meet the real Black Jack in any case. He put it aside and began to scan the old court records. For a man who'd started working for the outfit that owned Julesburg, he'd sure spent a lot of time in court.

Most of his troubles were for disturbing the peace or

hurting someone less than mortal, of course. The bestial slow killing of Jules Beñe had earned him a good scolding by the county coroner, but nobody seemed to have the balls to swear out a warrant on him for what could only be described as the cold-blooded torture and murder of a bound and helpless victim, no matter how mad a man had the right to be at Beñe for their earlier shootout. Longarm was mildly surprised to learn that Slade's wife had in fact been named Virginia. He guessed a lady named Virginia had a right to visit Virginia City, when you studied on it. The reason they'd left for there, according to the county, was twofold. Someone had finally got up the gumption to swear out a warrant charging Slade with assaulting a Julesburg citizen with intent to kill. About the same time, Slade had gotten into a fuss with an officer out at Fort Halleck and shot the post up without killing anybody. The *younger* killer's bite was worse than that of the man he so admired.

Longarm made a mental note that both warrants had been sworn out by the State of Colorado, even though the one misdeed had taken place on army property. The army hadn't always had fools like Colonel Walthers running its military police.

There was a follow-up report by the posse who'd chased Black Jack and even his wife out of their jurisdiction. The fugitive couple had followed the main branch of the Overland Trail due west through a corner of Nebraska and a lot more of Wyoming by the time the posse decided they were stretching the doctrine of hot pursuit past common sense and dropped back across the Colorado line. It said, here, they assumed he'd been headed for the south pass when last they'd cut his sign. With the advantage of hindsight, Longarm knew they'd turned north this side of the great divide and gone north so the Montana vigilantes could take care of the dumb brute. There wasn't a thing to suggest the model of

Black Jack Junior had ever done anything slick and sneaky. He'd just run loose like a mad dog until somebody killed him. He hadn't even changed his name when he got to Montana. He'd *bragged* about all the things he'd done in other parts until they'd strung him up. The only mysterious thing the real Black Jack had done was to get buried way out in Salt Lake on his way to get buried in Illinois. There wasn't anything in the old Sedgwick County records about that. One got the distinct impression Sedgwick County had never wanted to see Black Jack again and, since they'd had their way, Longarm closed their file and just sat there, stumped, as he pondered what he might do next if he was playing Black Jack Slade.

The pretty redhead came back in with a couple of mugs of coffee, saying, "I forgot to ask if you took cream and sugar. I like mine black. It keeps me peppy at night."

He rose to give back her seat and take his cup as he told her he liked to stay peppy, too. "If you was crazy and had your choice between heading for Utah or Montana, which way would you go, ma'am?" he asked.

"Call me Rita. At this time of the year I'd go up to Montana and hope it was cooler. If it was winter I'd head for Utah, where it doesn't snow so hard. What are we talking about, Deputy Long?"

He smiled. "Call me Custis, Miss Rita. We are trying to figure the mind of a kid whose mind, so far, seems sort of scrambled. He thinks he's reliving the life of a long-dead killer and, to give him his due, so far he's been acting even worse. As of the moment, he's got James Butler Hickock beat, and he's been at it no more than forty-eight hours."

"I heard them talking about the killings out at Fort Halleck. But surely you're joking about Wild Bill?"

He inhaled some of the black bitter brew and said, "Unlike some reporters, or old Jim himself, coroner's juries don't count pistol whippings or even wingings as killings. Jim never aimed to kill when he was sober, and his aim wasn't so good when he was drunk. He was *wild* enough, but despite all the fights he got into, or said he had, he was only recorded as the direct cause of a death four or five times. It took him over fifteen years to kill *that* many, solo and serious. Black Jack has gunned more gents than that in just a few days. So you tell me who's been acting wild around here."

She said, "Another time, perhaps. I can't get out of here until I finish a mess of deed recordings, and I sure want to get out of here this evening."

He said he was sorry, finished the coffee, and picked up the old folder. She told him just to leave it atop the filing cabinet, so he did. But as he was leaving she suddenly blurted, as if she'd been trying to hold it in, "I should be through here in about two hours, if you'd care to walk me home. I'd love to hear more about your quest, and my place isn't half as stuffy as this office."

He cursed inwardly as he saw that no matter how he answered he was going to make at least one Julesburg gal mad as hell. This one was younger, prettier, and likely less used to being let down by life. Myrtle would be less surprised but more hurt.

He was trying to come up with a graceful way to refuse what had to be the better offer, from a selfish point of view, when he was saved by the sound of gunshots close outside.

He dashed out of the county clerk's office and down the long corridor for the front entrance. Others were dashing the same way, and he heard someone shouting something about a shooting in the Majestic Saloon. That was where he'd left Smiley and Dutch, so he ran even faster, gun in hand, all the way.

As he burst into the saloon he saw the crowd was standing around the still form of the late Sergeant Fagan. Fagan had changed into a checked suit and personal buscadero gun rig. His army issue revolver reposed in the sawdust at his side. In addition to his earlier injuries at Longarm's hand and boot, he had a little blue hole in his forehead.

Longarm saw Smiley and Dutch standing sort of alone in the crowd, trying to look innocent. He stepped over the dead man to join them, growling, "All right. Which one of you did he call a son of a bitch?"

Dutch said, "Neither. He called *you* a son of a bitch," and added modestly, "He'd have *really* wound up hurt had he called *me* a son of a bitch."

Smiley said, "I'm a witness for the defense. The one on the floor stormed in drunk and loaded for bear just now. He roared out that he was looking for you, and named you just as rudely as old Dutch says. Dutch stepped away from the bar in his usual courteous manner and chided him for speaking so uncouth about a peace officer. The idjet went for his gun without further discussion. He was good. He might have taken anyone who wasn't as fast as Dutch. But, as you can plainly see, he just wasn't as good as he thought he might be."

A couple of townees in the crowd chimed in to back Smiley's words. One man offered the opinion that Sergeant Fagan had been asking for what he got before Dutch ever gave it to him.

Longarm still rolled his eyes heavenward and told them both they'd acted dumb as hell. "You could have just kept still and let some *other* idjet deal with him. This world is full of such idjets. Now you're both stuck here pending a hearing and Lord knows how many forms to fill out."

Dutch insisted defensively, "Hell, we couldn't just leave him be, after he told us right out he was gunning for you, could we?"

"I know you meant well, Dutch," Longarm said, "but this ain't the first time I've told you to leave my fighting to me. For one thing, I've a much sweeter disposition."

"You'd have had to gun this one," Smiley said flatly, "he was crazy-mean drunk and, drunk or sober, *fast*. He got that gun out after Dutch had already killed him."

Dutch nodded. "That's why I had to shoot him so much. It was the head shot as finally made him lose interest in me. He was so mad and so drunk he didn't seem to notice getting hit all over the rest of him. It's rare to see a man stay on his feet with even *one* .44-40 in him. But he was one tough hombre, with the body weight to soak up the shock."

An older man with a harassed look and a golden star pinned to his vest bulled through to join them, sighing, "Aw, shit, I *knew* this cuss wasn't long for this world, but we're still going to have a fuss with Uncle Sam about this. He was *army,* cuss his hide. Who gunned him? I don't have to ask *why*."

Longarm introduced himself and his sidekicks, and Dutch owned up to the shooting without any prompting. "It was pure self-defense, in front of friendly witnesses, and you are *talking* to Uncle Sam. All three of us is federal."

The county law looked worried. "I fear I'm going to have to bind you over to the coroner just the same, and I hope you all notice I ain't bearing arms. I just come from an after-supper lie-down and Lord knows where my fool wife hung my guns."

Longarm said, "You can't hold me and Smiley. We didn't do it."

But Smiley said, "I ain't leaving here without my little pard. I *would* have shot the bastard if Dutch hadn't beat me to it. He was asking for what he got, and I mean to witness that for old Dutch. So where do we go from here, Sheriff?"

The county law told them he saw no need to lock up

fellow peace officers, as long as he had their word they'd stick around until the coroner's jury decided to let them go or bound them over to the grand jury, which hardly seemed likely.

Longarm was about to say he'd sit in, too. But then a kid from the telegraph office pushed through the crowd, gulped as he saw what they were all crowded around, and handed a wire to the sheriff.

The older man muttered, tore it open, and read it before he said, "Aw, hell, Lord, that just ain't fair. I got enough on my plate right now. You didn't have to serve me this as well."

Longarm asked what was wrong. The sheriff said, "Another damn killing. But hold on. I don't see why they tried to hand this one to us. It didn't even occur in Colorado, let alone my county."

"Who got killed where, then, Sheriff?"

"Blacksmith up in Scott's Bluff, Nebraska. Looks like it was done by that same little rascal with the fancy chaps. I sure hope it was. That means we're rid of him."

Longarm sighed. "Speak for yourself." Then he turned to Smiley. "You're going to have to wire Billy anyhow. You can save me some time by adding that our want is following the north fork of the Overland Trail, like I hoped he would, and that I'm on my way the same way."

"Billy sent us to back your play. You can't go on *alone*," Smiley objected.

"Sure I can. Just watch me. By the time you boys untangle your fool selves, here, I hope to have the little bastard, dead or alive. Tell Billy I'll try to wire from Scott's Bluff. I got some complicated railroading to work out."

He left before anyone could figure out how to stop him, and legged it back to the hotel. He'd left his saddle and possibles in the stable with Blue Boy in case of more local travel in a hurry. So he could have gotten clear without saying adios to old Myrtle.

He was tempted. Weepy women were a pain. But he knew that, even if he never had to watch her weeping, she figured to feel even more used and abused if he just sneaked out on her. So he toted his gear inside, where Myrtle was minding her desk again and, as she saw he was carrying his luggage, she looked kicked in the belly more than weepy.

He told her, "It ain't the way it might look, honey. I was sure looking forward to the sound of them bedsprings upstairs, but I just got a line on that young killer. I got to try and stop him before he kills again. This time he ain't got as good a lead on me, but he's still got a good one. So I got to go, and I don't want you to take my hasty departing personal, hear?"

She stared soberly down at the saddle braced on his hip and said, "You could have left by the back way, at least, you brute."

"That could have been took more brutal. I figured I owed a pretty lady a proper parting of the ways," he told her.

She looked blank at first. Then she smiled radiantly. "I'll be damned if I don't think you *meant* that, and you've made my day in more ways than one, even if the night ahead promises to be an awful letdown. God bless you, Custis Long, and try to remember me the next time you're back this way. For I doubt I'll ever forget *you* and the all-too-short time you made me feel so young and pretty again."

He leaned across to kiss her and promised to visit, should he ever pass through Julesburg again. Then he got away before she could blubber up on him. He knew that last part had been a lie, even if it had been a white lie. He passed through Julesburg often enough on more serious business. But he knew it was best to break clean, with even good-looking women, if one wanted a clear conscience and pleasant memories. He figured a lot of good old gals he recalled wistfully enjoyed their soft place in his heart because he'd had to move on before they'd felt free to nag him about the way he just was. He wanted to remember Myrtle as a sweet old gal. So it was just as well there were other places to stay in Julesburg, if he ever got stuck here overnight again.

He'd memorized the local timetable, so he wasn't surprised when he heard a distant locomotive moan at a crossing off to the east. He legged it to the depot, put his saddle on an empty baggage cart, and started to light a cheroot as he noticed there were seven other gents on the platform with him. He took them for fellow travelers until his match light glinted on the dress sword one of them had hanging down his blue pants. The same match lit Longarm's face, of course, so the one with the sword marched over to say, "They told us we might find you here, Deputy Long. You can forget about that west-bound train."

Longarm shook out his light and said, "Evening, Colonel Walthers. Ain't your corporal's squad two men short?"

Lieutenant Colonel Walthers, U.S. Army Military Police, was a man about Longarm's age and shape, in an army where fifty-year-old captains were not considered rare. Walthers was said to boot-lick his superiors with the same enthusiasm he bullied his inferiors, which included ninety-nine percent of the human race, to hear old Walthers talk. "You have to come back to Fort Halleck with us, Long. We're holding a board of inquiry on the death of Sergeant Fagan," he said.

Longarm said, "That's the army's business, not mine. I was nowhere near the idjet when he decided to commit suicide by slapping leather on a man *I'd* hate to mess with that way. There ain't no mystery for the army to solve. Your sergeant went down in front of a saloon full of witnesses, and the gent who gunned him has owned up to it. I'm headed for Scott's Bluff on a more important and less lawful shooting. So don't mess with me. I mean it."

But the officer told him, "I'm holding you responsible for Sergeant Fagan's death. I mean that, too."

Longarm snorted in disgust. "You know, every time I figure I know just how dumb you are, you have to prove me wrong by acting even dumber. This ain't a beauty contest between you and me. You'd be pretty as hell if you wiped that constant smirk off your fool face. We're both after a man who kills soldiers a lot more regular than old Dutch. He just murdered a civilian, for a change, in Scott's Bluff. If you and your boys would rather stay here and pick nits about an open-and-shut case that can only go one way, that's up to you. I see my train coming in now. It's been nice talking to you."

He picked up his saddle with his left hand and took a step toward the tracks. Walthers stepped into his path, stuck his chest out at him, and snapped, "If you won't come willingly we'll just have to disarm and handcuff you. Lieutenant Parsons, arrest this civilian!"

The U.P. westbound combo was rolling to a stop behind Walthers. Longarm clamped down on his cheroot with bared teeth, balled up his right fist, and planted it in Walther's superior smile, hard.

The short-colonel went down, his face a bloody ruin, as the nearest shavetail gasped in awe and said, "You can't do that!"

Longarm drew his six-gun with the same lethal fist. "I just did. Before anyone else gets hurt, I want you boys to add up the odds here and . . . Keep that gun hand *polite*, Trooper. I *mean* it!"

The enlisted man who'd just unsnapped the flap of his holster had noticed Longarm seemed to be a man who meant it, when he said he meant it. So he froze, looking sort of sick.

Longarm threw his saddle aboard the nearest rail car's loading platform, but kept them all covered. He smiled thinly and said, "That's better. I know it's six of you to five rounds in this wheel. So I know at least one of you would surely nail me no matter how the other five made out. I'm only human. For all we know, I might not take all five down with me. So place your bets and let the game commence."

Nobody moved or said a word, save for Walthers himself, who was rolling about on the platform with both hands to his face, demanding they arrest his attacker.

Longarm climbed the steps backward, gun muzzle trained on the sullen but smart soldiers. After a few tense, awkward seconds the locomotive up ahead sounded its whistle, the platform under him jerked into motion, and Longarm was on his way west.

As he holstered his gun and picked up his saddle, a conductor Longarm knew came out to join him, saying, "Evening, Longarm. You don't have to show me your U.P. pass. I've seen it often enough. What was that all about back there? It sounded sort of serious."

Longarm shrugged. "I reckon they weren't as serious as me, after all."

Chapter 9

Following the Overland or any other old wagon trail by rail was complicated. Rolling west the hard way, the pioneers had been more anxious about getting there alive than getting there in a hurry. The old trails had been laid out with water and easy pulling in mind, following streambeds and avoiding steep grades as often as possible.

The stage lines that followed the first covered wagons had tried to sell more speed to both passengers and the post office. So while the Overland Trail had to more or less follow the trend of the earlier Oregon and Mormon trails, it tended to cut across river bends and top more rises with its lighter coaches.

The railroad builders had wanted to sell even more speed and, having machinery and black powder to work with, they'd taken even more direct routes, bridging, grading, and tunneling to beeline where nothing pulled by draft animals could have gone. The U.P. had saved on miles of expensive steel tracks by using cheaper immigrant labor to bull through the Rockies well south of the easier, traditional passes. The older stage route had of course made the wider swing to the north. So, when his train got to Sidney, Longarm and his gear got off to catch the short line up to Northport, Nebraska, and catch another U.P. the thirty-odd miles northwest to Scott's Bluff.

You couldn't see the cliffs the town was named after this late at night. It was hard to see much of the town, now that the oil lamps along the main street were all that seemed awake enough to matter. He left his modest luggage checked in at the depot and headed for the local branch of the sheriff's department. Despite its name and former fame, Scott's Bluff had lost out when they'd got around to choosing the county seat. So the sheriff's office there was run by a senior deputy, while the elected official he ran it for got to sleep in Gering on the far side of the North Platte.

The senior deputy had gone home for the night, too. But the crusty old gent left to mind the office and keep an eye on the drunks in the tank knew Longarm by reputation and got up out of his rocking chair to shake and say, "We was expecting some federal men. Did you know the army has just sworn out a warrant on you and wired us to arrest you on sight?"

"I didn't. But it don't surprise me. Are you figuring on arresting me, sir?" Longarm asked.

"Call me Jeff. Hell, no. You never beat up no short-colonels in *Nebraska*. You'd think a man smart enough to make short-colonel would know better than to ask Nebraska to arrest a man on a Colorado fistfight."

Longarm chuckled. "Old Walthers ain't smart enough to make assistant squad leader. But I come up here to talk about more important pests, if it's all the same with you."

Old Jeff nodded and said, "I'd be proud to show you the scene of the crime. It's just down the way, across from a saloon that stays open late. We let the dead man's kin carry his body home to wake, once the doc who fills in for the coroner here examined it some, of course. There was no mystery about the cause of death. He'd been shot direct in the center of his forehead, at close range. Lord knows how the undertaker means to get them powder burns off, if they mean to hold an open-casket service. The horse has been impounded as evidence. Meaning it's in the corral out back. They didn't require us to talk so fancy in the old days, and we still hung the right gents, most of the time."

"I've noticed that. You say you have a *horse* for me to look at?" Longarm asked.

Old Jeff shrugged. "You can if you like. I doubt it will be able to tell you much. Horses don't talk, you know."

Longarm said they'd see about that and the old town law led him out back where, sure enough, a big part-thoroughbred bay was alone in the smaller pole corral next to the bigger one the town law used for its own remuda.

Old Jeff called to it and it came over to have its muzzle patted. "He's a friendly critter, considering who rid him into town from Lord knows where," Jeff remarked. "Our riders wasn't able to read sign on the baked prairie. We got the saddle and bridle in the tack room. Both army. Like the horse. The boss says that don't prove it's the officer's mount the kid stole. But the brute is packing an army remount service brand and I can't come up with a better notion where he might have picked it up. Come on, I'll show you where the murderous little bastard abandoned it."

They cut through a vacant lot, back to the main street, and the scene of the crime was only a few doors down. The interior of the open-front smithy was dark until Jeff lit an oil lamp hanging above the anvil by the cold forge. Longarm saw that the more portable tools of the dead blacksmith's trade had been put away for safe keeping, kids being kids, and some grownups being worse.

Old Jeff pointed with his chin. "The smith was ahint the anvil and the killer was standing just this side of it, as we put it together. The kid must have shoved his .45 across the anvil direct in the smith's poor face and pulled the trigger, once."

Longarm grimaced. "Where did you find his army mount?" he asked.

The older lawman said, "Outside, running loose, after. But it left hoofmarks in here, first. It reads that young Slade led it in, got into some sort of fuss with the smith, and blowed his brains out."

Longarm asked, "Has anyone thought to examine the feet of that witness?"

The answer was, "Sure. We may be small-town, but we ain't stupid. That couldn't have been what they was arguing about. The critter is still wearing well-nailed iron, as shows the same trail wear. Aside from that, the wagon spring the smith was fixing when he died was still too hot to pick up when someone tried. It sure do make one wonder. But then, the fliers we got on the fugitive *said* he was *crazy*. So there's just no way us saner gents can figure what they was arguing about."

Longarm nodded and said, "The wire *I* got said the killer was seen by local witnesses. That hardly jibes with what you just told me, no offense."

"None taken. Nobody witnessed the exact killing, but they sure heard the gunshot across the street. At that time of evening there was nothing open around here but the smithy, open late, and the saloon across the way. The sound attracted the attention of the serious drinkers at the bar, and most of 'em stepped out on the board-walk for a look-see. What they seen was a stubby little cuss in flapping fur chaps and black Texas hat coming their way, waving two guns and saying mean things about all their mothers. So they went back inside, sudden."

Longarm said that sounded reasonable. "What happened then?"

Old Jeff said, "What happened was that Clovis Sinclair as rides for the X Slash X lost a fifty-dollar saddle and a fifteen-dollar pony. The stubby-legged killer must not have felt up to chasing the horse he rid in on. So he helped hisself to the cow pony and lit out of town, crowing like a rooster and shooting at the stars. Old Clovis is mad as hell. Aside from losing his show-off saddle, he has to pay for the pony the X Slash X let him ride to town. Them's the rules, when you lose your employer's stock."

Longarm said he knew that and asked what the more recently stolen horseflesh looked like. Old Jeff replied, "Scrub buckskin with no blazes and a black mane and tail. Branded X Slash X, of course. The saddle would be easier to I.D. from a distance. It's a black double-rig Vadelia, mounted with what Clovis says is silver. He wouldn't know real silver from German-silver, but then, neither would I from a dozen yards off. By now the little fool as stole it could be showing it off most anywhere."

"I hope not. I've reason to suspect he's riding the old Overland Trail on a lunatic's quest. The big question is whether he means to leave it east of the South Pass and head north to get lynched some more, or follow the trail west to Salt Lake City and put flowers on his own grave."

Old Jeff said, "What you just said might make sense to *you,* old son, but it sounds sort of silly to me, unless I missed something."

Longarm said, "That's fair. Black Jack Junior has been *thinking* mighty silly. But, either way, he'd have to follow the old trail, some."

"Well, he has a good lead on you, but it's a good

week or ten days' ride to the south pass country, and that long-legged army mount he left here looks a lot faster than the scrub buckskin he swapped it for," Jeff observed. "So if you want to impound it as your own federal evidence . . ."

"No thanks," Longarm cut in. "The *iron* horse is even faster. As I read the timetable, I can catch a midnight combo up as far as Bonneville Junction and get there by morning. There's a mountain local from there as far south as Saint Stephens, where the tracks and me begin to disagree as to where we're headed. If I beg, borrow, or buy a mount *there*, I can follow Beaver Creek an easy two days' ride and beat the little rascal to the South Pass with so much time to spare I'll likely wind up bored as hell before it gets exciting."

Old Jeff thought and said, "That sure sounds boring, it's true. Why not just take the the U.P. transcontinental and get off where it *crosses* the South Pass?"

"It does and it doesn't. What everyone today thinks of as the South Pass ain't what that colored mountain man, Sublette, mapped out when he was the first to find that way over the Divide. Some Indians showed him how flat their Shining Mountains got just south of Atlantic Peak. So he followed *their* trial and dubbed it the South Pass because it was south of the way Lewis and Clark had said they'd found the only passage. It took a spell for others to notice that whole stretch of mountains was more like rolling prairie for a good hundred miles north and south. Meanwhile, all sorts of folk had followed Sublette's map and left wagon ruts where the map said the official South Pass was. It's still the best *wagon* trace, if you got plenty of time, and like to stick close to water and firewood off the slopes to the north. The railroad was in more of a hurry and ran its line way south of the trail laid out by Sublette, Brigham Young, and such. The Overland coaches followed the older, longer route. Atlantic City and South Pass City, whilst hardly cities, are still in business, even if Overland Express ain't. I figure a lunatic who thinks he's a hired gun for Overland Express will follow their old route. If I took the railroad and got off, say, in Bitter Creek, I'd have to ride *farther* to cut him off, see?"

Old Jeff said, "I'm sure glad you ain't trailing *me*. It ain't fixing to be midnight for quite a spell, and Lord knows what the Northern Division of the U.P. will be serving as food and drink by the time she shows up, with all the ice long melted. So what say we cross the street to treat our bellies better?"

"I could sure do with some ham and eggs. But what about the prisoners back there in your tank, Jeff?" Longarm asked.

The older lawman said, "Let 'em get their own grub. None of 'em are in for anything more serious than acting drunk and disgusting, anyway. Do they all escape, it'll save the judge the tiresome chore of cussing 'em out and letting 'em go in the morning."

Longarm allowed it was old Jeff's town and they went across to the saloon. The boss there said he never argued with the law but asked them if they'd mind eating in the kitchen lest the others out front want some, too.

They agreed and were seated at a kitchen table, finishing up with apple pie washed down with beer, when it got sort of noisy out front. So they got up to go see what the fuss was all about.

A young cowhand was orating from one end of the bar, upon which sat a black and silver mounted Vadelia show saddle. They joined him and made him start all over again. He didn't seem to mind. He struck a heroic pose and declared, "I was riding in off the Circle H when a pack of growlsome coyotes spooked my pony. As I got him back down outten the stars I seen something glinting at me from the dark, about fifty yards offen the wagon trace. I knew it had to be a coyote's eye. So I shot it. When it never even blinked I shot it again and, when it was *still* there, I knew either me or my saddle gun had to be wrong. So I got down and moved in on it for a closer look-see."

He paused for dramatic effect and another swig of beer before he continued. "It was the silver horn of this here saddle I was trying to shoot for a coyote and, lucky for Clovis Sinclair, I'd only grazed it once. It was still cinched to that buckskin Clovis lost right out front the other night. Someone had shot it in the head and buried it under tumbleweed to make it look like a big old clump of brush against a bobwire fence. I had to laugh as I thought about how the posse must have rid right past it more than once."

Old Jeff said, "You always did talk fresh to your elders. The critter was doubtless hid a lot better before them coyotes got to nosing the tumbleweed aside to get at the stale meat, as coyotes tend to do. But I reckon you're entitled to your brag. For you just saved Longarm, here, a needless as well as long train ride."

Longarm shook his head. "Not hardly. I see no need to change my plans worth mention."

Old Jeff frowned up at him and asked, "How come? Young Slade could hardly be meaning to follow the old Overland Trail aboard that buckskin, if he shot and hid it right outside of town."

"Sure he could. He established by his earlier actions that night that he didn't like to walk far. He knew the well-known mount he grabbed for a hasty exit was easier than many a pony to recognize at a distance. So, having cleared the city limits, he got rid of it."

Old Jeff said, "Anyone can see that, now. What did he do then, start walking in his flappy chaps?"

"Not hardly. He moves around too good on them stubby legs for a walking man. You boys would have *caught* him if he'd been *that* crazy. He rode out to where

116

he'd left *another* mount tied up, likely to that same bob-wire fence."

There was a collective gasp of admiration from the crowd. Old Jeff warned them, "Don't never try to get away from *this* old boy." But then he asked Longarm, "What kind of other horse are we talking about? The only mount stole this side of the county line was the buckskin he shot and left for the coyotes, close."

"I wish you hadn't asked that, Jeff. I like to look smart. But lots of serious travelers travel with two mounts, so's they can change from one to the other and make better time. Let's say *he* was moving that way. He tied his spare mount outside town and rode in on the other to scout the same. He found the smithy open and went in to ask the smith something. Don't ask me what. A halfway sane man might not be able to offer a guess. The smith was one of us saner gents. So when Black Jack Junior asked him some crazy question the smith might have said it was a crazy question and, however politely put, drove the lunatic even crazier. I have seen the results of his hair-trigger temper before."

Old Jeff nodded. "All right. I can read her from there. He gunned the smith, lit out aboard the buckskin, and... Hold on. It gets even crazier. Didn't you say you thought he was trying to follow the old Overland Trail out to some graveyard, Longarm?"

Longarm nodded and the older lawman said, "You're following him the wrong way. Why would a man headed west along the old trail tether a horse north*west* of a town he aimed to scout before riding through to the south*east* if he aimed to go west?"

The youth who'd brought in the saddle opined, "He could be *lost,* if he's loco," and there was a murmur of agreement.

Longarm thought. "If there's one thing that mad killer is keeping track of it's the Overland Trail. Try her this way. Say he rode in from the southeast, following his shining path where it turns into your main street for a spell. Say he passed the smithy, open late, saw the smith was alone and unarmed at his forge, and then rode on out the far side, tethered his getaway ride, and came back to do his dirty deed?"

Old Jeff gulped. "You mean premeditated? A man he'd never seen before? A man who couldn't have given him any sane reason to even cuss at?"

Longarm nodded grimly. "Why not? He's *crazy*, ain't he?

Old Jeff swore softly. "That's pushing past crazy into mad-dog vicious, if you don't mind saying so."

Longarm said, "I don't mind. It's likely true."

Chapter 10

By the time Longarm got off the freight train he'd managed to hop as far as Saint Stephens after a series of slow rides on even less comfortable rolling stock, Longarm was hungry as a wolf again. He toted his saddle and possibles across the cinder-paved main and only street to a shed advertising itself as a Café de Paris. The waitress behind the counter was nice-looking, but after that any possible resemblance to the real Paris evaporated in the thin, dry mountain morning air. She served him greasy hash topped with what smelled like a buzzard's egg, over-fried, and a mug of coffee that tasted like bile even over-sweetened with sugar and canned cow. He was so hungry he didn't feel up to wrecking the joint, and the pretty waitress was so relieved, she smiled at him.

He smiled back and after he'd introduced himself he asked her if she knew where he could buy a horse. She nodded and said, "Sure. Livestock is a lot easier to come by up this way than decent coffee. Try Pop Roberts an easy stroll down the tracks. He's got the corral down that way. Tell him Ruby sent you. That's me, Ruby Perkins, and I get off at six this evening."

He assured her he'd keep that in mind and, since he doubted he'd be anywhere near at six, he tipped her a whole quarter, lest she feel he didn't admire her batty eyelashes.

The awful breakfast made him feel better and, along with the crisp, cool air up here, put more spring in his legs as he toted his riding gear ever onward in hopes of finding something worth putting it on.

Pop Roberts turned out to be a friendly old cuss who agreed young Ruby was a pretty little thing, even if she was sort of stupid, and said he'd be proud to sell the U.S. government a horse, since that was what he raised them for. The conversation got a mite less friendly as they looked over the stock in the corral, and the old man tried to tell Longarm a wall-eyed paint with scarred flanks was just the critter to carry a man his size.

Longarm said, "I can see he's barrel-chested enough to have fair wind at this altitude. But how come he's so scarred up from scraping corners, likely moving sudden?"

Pop Roberts looked innocent. "Well, to tell the truth, he don't *see* so good. But, as you say you're going up into the South Pass country, where trees and even fence-posts are few and far between—"

Longarm cut in, "They make me dress like this because I work for an administration that don't serve hard drink at the White House no more. But that don't mean I'm a *total* dude. I don't mean to brag, but I have done some riding in my time and, whenever possible, I've rid *horses,* not crowbait you couldn't sell to a greenhorn with a lick of common sense."

Pop soothed, "I can see by your boots and them bullet holes in your Stetson that you've been around, old son. How do you feel about that handsome black gelding yonder?"

Longarm said, "I've been around more than that. If he ain't spooky I'm in need of specs. What about that chestnut mare with the blaze and white socks? I like her lines, and she looks steady as well as frisky."

The sly old horse trader smiled despite himself. "You do know which end of a horse the shit falls from, don't you? That one will cost you. I've been saving her for a serious riding man."

"What do I look like, a ballerina?" Longarm asked. "I'll give you a quarter for her."

Pop said, "No you won't. That pretty little thing is worth six bits if she's worth a dollar, and you're still getting her for a steal because I'm so patriotic. I'd never part with her for less than a flat hundred if you was just another cowhand."

"Two bits. I just aim to ride her. I don't aim to make her the mother of my children and the solace of my old age, you know," Longarm said.

They argued back and forth until they finally settled on forty dollars and a handshake of mutual admiration. Pop Roberts roped the bay and hauled her out for Longarm to bridle and saddle. She didn't fight them. She looked like she was anxious to get out of there as well.

Once he was properly mounted, Longarm asked for directions to the nearest local law. The old horse trader sent him back the way he'd just come, the harder way. Longarm thanked him and rode back to such center as such a small town could be said to have. He dismounted, tethered the bay, whose name had turned out to be Ramona, and told her, "I like you, too, and I'll be right back as soon as I pay my dues to this friendly little town."

He strode into the lockup and town constabulary, and found yet another old gent dozing behind the desk. It seemed one had to be too old to move on, or too young and foolish to know better, if one meant to stay long in Saint Stephens. He introduced himself to the town law and gave him a quick rundown on his reasons for being this high above sea level. The old constable looked worried until Longarm told him, "I doubt Black Jack Junior will come your way. You ain't on the trail he admires so. But I thought it best to warn you it's possible, if he gets as smart as me about more modern forms of transportation. You know what he looks like and I want you to take it serious when I add that he's ten times more dangerous than your average Crooked Lancer on the warpath looks. So if he should come your way, shoot to kill, and then shoot him some more until his tail stops twitching."

The older and now more worried-looking lawman thanked him for his words of cheer. "I'll spread the word and tell even the preacher to strap on some hardware, like when the Shoshone went loco a few years back. You say you're trailing such a whale of destruction *alone*, Deputy Long?"

Longarm said, "I got to. But, what the hell, *he's* alone, too, and I've got an edge the others he's beat to the draw might not have. I *know* how sudden and crazy he can move."

"You mean to shoot to kill on sight, then?"

"I mean to try. I can only hope I'm good enough. I no longer care if it sounds fair. He'll try to kill *me* on sight. He's killed others that wasn't even armed. I'd feel worse gunning a mad dog in a schoolyard full of kids. A mad dog might have started out decent. The murderous little beast I'm after seems to have been no damned use as a child. He even hits women."

The old man behind the desk looked shocked. "In that case, put one in him for *me!* If he comes through here, we'll be ready for him. I'll tell the boys he hits women."

They shook on it and Longarm left, hoping his warning was just a caution and no more. He mounted up and rode southwest through scattered timber to where Beaver Creek crooked into the whitewater of the Little Popo Agie. He followed the wagon trace leading up the right bank of Beaver Creek even through he knew he'd have to ford it, higher up. The Beaver was whitewater, too, but not as ferocious as it could get. It was a lot cooler up this way in high summer, but just as dry as the high plains he'd come up from. For such rain clouds as came through this time of the year tended to trip over the higher peaks to the north and south.

A couple of miles outside of town, he watered Ramona where the wagon ruts swung closer to the Beaver and let her graze some while he dug into his possibles for more sensible trail wear. He sat in the shade of some lodgepole pines to change into blue jeans and matching work jacket. Then he stuffed the tobacco-brown tweeds they made him wear where other sissies could see him into his saddlebag, untethered Ramona, and mounted up to ride on a lot more sensible. He knew that from here on over into Mormon country he was unlikely to meet anyone who wouldn't laugh at a gent in a tweed suit. He knew that if he swung just a mite to the west as he rode southwest he'd be able to stop for a howdy at a certain cattle spread where he'd no doubt be offered a warm welcome. But he knew he shouldn't, so he knew he couldn't. It was likely just as well. Every time he and that pretty little Kim Stover got together for a spell they both wound up hurting. It wasn't the *kissing* of Kim Stover that hurt so bad. It was the *stopping* that hurt. For they always had to stop, even when he wasn't in this big a hurry, and save for a certain other blonde down Texas way, there was nobody he hated to stop kissing more.

He was tempted to lope his new mount. He could tell she was willing. But they had a good ride ahead, and if he was at all able to read a maniac's mind they had a good four or five days' lead on the real reason for all this traveling. He chuckled and told his mount, "You're sure lucky *your* kind ain't in heat all the time, like *my* kind seems to be. If I didn't know myself well enough to control myself so good, I'd run your ass ragged trying to kill two birds with one chestnut, and then I'd have *two* gals hating me in the end. Old Kim always swears she hates me when she can't get me to stay just a little longer, and Flora Banes is going to hate me for gunning her crazy kid brother, no matter how in the hell I explain it."

The mare didn't know what he was talking about so she saw no need to reply. He kept his thoughts to himself as he considered and rejected plan after plan for taking said brother alive. For, though he didn't give a damn about the feelings of a killer with no feelings about others, he knew poor little Flora was going to be upset as hell, even though even she had to know, deep down, that anyone who shot the silly little bastard would be doing her a favor.

Even if there was some way to take such a raving lunatic alive, there was no way in hell the docs could cure him. Longarm had read that even doctors smart enough to say what was wrong with a human brain in long German words admitted they had no cure for *total* lunatics. They could humor such a case who didn't seem out to *hurt* nobody. But what could anyone do with such a case once he took to killing folk for no sensible reason at all?

A cross-bill chirped at them from a nearby pine and Longarm said, "Aw, shut up, bird. A lot *you* know about the rotten chore they sent me to do."

He rode on and, after mulling it all over some more, decided, "All right, God damn it. I know I'm only a deputy, not a judge or a head doc. I'll *try* to deliver him alive, and let smarter gents than me decide what's to be done with him. But I sure wish I was smart enough to know how I was supposed to *do* that. Even if I get the drop on him, he don't figure to *listen*. The real Black Jack Slade never did. That's how come they had to kill him to stop *him,* too."

He tried to get his mind on something more cheerful than Kim Stover's nice build or Black Jack Junior's disgusting ways, knowing neither could be within reach for quite a few miles. But his mind kept swinging back to one or the other as he rode on and on.

A good five miles up the trail, he spotted a figure running down it towards him. He saw it was a boy of about fourteen, barefoot and wearing nothing but bib overalls. The poor kid's feet had both been cut on sharp pebbles or glass he'd run over, and he was bleeding like hell from a cut across the forehead as well. Longarm reined in. The kid ran past him as if he hadn't been there.

Longarm blinked in surprise and heeled Ramona after the running wonder. Catching up was easy enough. But since Longarm didn't carry a throw rope on his McClellan saddle, he had to lean out and grab the running boy by the X of his overall straps.

Longarm reined in again, saying, "Hold still, damn it. I'm on your side, whatever the hell you're running from."

He dismounted, on the off side, as the kid kept trying to run on, blubbering, "Lemme go! Lemme go! My mom's hurt bad and I gotta git the doc!"

Longarm shook him to plant him in one spot. "You ain't fixing to make town on them feet, now, boy. Simmer down and tell me what happened and how far."

The boy sobbed, "Pappy licked her bad, with a loop of bobwire. I tried to stop him but he licked *me,* too. When I was able to stop him she was lying all over the

125

floor, bleeding all over, with her dress tore half off. I think she's dead. I got to go get the doc in case she ain't."

Longarm growled deep in his throat. "Judging by that slice the bobwire took out of your face, we could be talking more blood than fatal injuries. I'm handy at stopping bleeding, and no doubt she's bled more than she really ought to by now. So we're going back, riding double. Because you can't run much further and I don't know the way. Hear?"

The boy seemed to see him for the first time. He sobbed, "You can help her, mister? You can keep Mom from dying?"

Longarm didn't know, so he didn't answer. He remounted and hauled the kid up behind him, and if it wasn't comfortable atop a bedroll, it still beat running or even walking on torn-up bare feet.

Knowing which direction the kid had been running from, Longarm rode them that way a spell before he asked, "Do you want to tell me where we're going, or would you rather I just guessed?"

The kid told him to swing left at the next fork. When they topped a gentle rise, and Longarm saw wagon ruts through the grass running in to join the main trail, he did so. The grass was taller and greener at this altitude. The tracks led across the bottomlands of the Beaver to run between two big granite outcrops. Then they were in a shallow dell, surrounded by more rimrock, and occupied by a mighty lazy homesteader's notion of an improved claim.

The cabin and outbuildings had been thrown up sort of cockeyed, with as little labor as possible, and skinny logs even a weakling could chop through with a few blows. Plank roofing like that was supposed to be shingled or at least sodded unless one enjoyed cold unexpected showers every time it really got to raining, and up here it was only dry *most* of the time, not *all* the time. It was the wrong time of the year to worry about cabin chinking, so Longarm didn't comment on cross-ventilation as they rode in. He asked the kid behind him where they might expect to find the man of the house, and in what condition.

The boy said, "I reckon he's dead. I had to make him stop."

Longarm thought that over before he asked quietly, "How did you stop him, son?"

"With an axe. There was one by the fireplace and when he knocked me headfirst into the kindling wood, I just come up swinging what was handy."

Longarm whistled softly. "Well, a boy has to protect his mom, I reckon. How come your old man was acting so ornery in the first place?"

"I don't know. Neither of us had done nothing to make him mad. But when Pappy got to drinking, he didn't need much excuse. I was out back milking the goat when I hear Mom screaming for mercy. When I run into the cabin Pappy had her on the floor as he went after her with that whip he'd made of bobwire. I took holt of his arm and begged him to stop, but he hit me with it as well. I tried to grab him again and he back-handed me clear over the table into the fireplace. That's when I come back at him serious with the axe. Do you reckon they're going to hang me for hitting Pappy with that axe, mister?"

Longarm shook his head. "Not if your mother lives to back your words, son." He reined in by the wide-open cabin door and added, "She's what we got to worry about now. Justifiable homicide can always wait until the law gets around to it."

They dismounted and went inside. The interior smelled clean despite the chinks of daylight showing through the log walls and the stale scent of boiled greens.

There was only one body on the rammed dirt floor. It

was moaning. Longarm stepped over the axe on the floor between them and hunkered down to see what needed to be done.

The badly beaten woman was a once-pretty woman of, say, thirty-five. Had she been living more civilized he'd have figured her for fifty. Her cheap calico mother-hubbard was so torn it made it easy to examine her without asking the patient to undress. The multiple lacerations from the bobwire she'd been lashed with had stopped bleeding and were starting to scab over. Lacking a quart or two of iodine, Longarm figured it best to count on the early bleeding having washed any lockjaw bugs out of the shallow wounds, and scabs would do as much or more for her than picking them open and fussing with them.

He gently opened one eyelid and held a lit match near the dilated pupil a moment before he told the boy in the doorway, "The whipping didn't do her as much damage as the jar her skull seems to have taken, whether from a fist or from hitting the floor."

The kid's voice pleaded more than it asked, "Is she gonna be all right, mister?"

Longarm said, "I don't know. It would take a real doc to say. She's suffering shock and concussion. I've seen folk in this condition recover natural and I've seen it go worse. Where's the nearest doctor? I know there's no damn hospital in the village I just rode out of."

The boy said he'd been running for the local midwife, who'd had some training as a hospital nurse one time.

"I reckon she'd know more than me," Longarm said, "so here's what I want you to do. I want you to go out and get my Winchester saddle gun, saddlebags, and possibles roll. After you bring 'em in here I want you to fork that mare and ride for that medicine lady. What are you waiting for, boy? *Do* it!"

The kid gulped, ran out of sight, and was back by the

time Longarm had rummaged about, found some much-mended but clean wool socks, and pulled the injured woman's skirts down neater. As the boy piled Longarm's gear on the dirt beside them he asked, "Did you want this rifle gun because you're afraid Pappy ain't really dead?"

"The thought had crossed my mind. Men killed entire with an axe hardly ever get up and go somewhere else. So it seems safe to assume you hit him with the flat of the blade, however hard you tried to split his skull. Was your old man armed with anything more serious than bobwire when last you noticed?"

The boy looked around and said, "I don't see the shotgun he had over the fireplace, before."

"All right. Get going. Don't you *want* your mother to make it?" Longarm asked.

The kid vanished from view and a few moments later Longarm could tell from the fading sounds of Ramona's hooves that he was headed somewhere fast.

Longarm unrolled his bedding beside the battered wife. As he was gently sliding her atop the ground cloth she murmured, "What are you doing, Dan?"

He didn't know whether Dan was her kid or her man. He didn't care. He told her, reassuringly, "I'm putting you to bed, ma'am. You're in shock and we got to get your body warmer and your head cooler."

She didn't answer. In her semi-conscious state she couldn't understand his words, but they seemed to have a calming effect on her.

Chapter 11

Longarm covered the woman with his blankets and rain tarp. Then he wet the old socks with canteen water and wrapped them around her skull like a clumsy gray bandage. He poured more water over the wool once he had her head still again. As he did so he saw the tip of her tongue moving between her pale lips. He took out his kerchief, wet that cloth, too, and let her suck on it some.

There was nothing else he could really do for her. He rose with his Winchester at port to see what else needed doing in these parts. He levered a round in the chamber and ducked out the door and to one side, fast, as he scanned the surrounding scenery. The only thing moving in his line of sight was a scrawny chicken pecking at a fresh horse apple Ramona had left in the dust of the dooryard. Longarm grimaced and said, "Yeah, a lazy nester can save feeding you birds regular if he lets you rustle your own grub, even if you do wind up sort of stringy. Those of you as ain't eaten by varmints, I mean."

He circled around to the back, ready for anything. He was still surprised at how run-down the layout was, despite how fresh the bark on the unstripped bark of the mostly lodgepole pine construction looked. The out-buildings and corral on this untidy spread were already turning to punkwood. But he was more worried about punks inside the sheds than the condition of their flimsy walls. So he examined them all with care.

He found the goat milking stand the kid had mentioned in one shed. Where the goat or goats had run off to was anybody's guess. He saw more chickens grubbing in the grass all about. They didn't seem to have any other livestock. But he found some badly smoked beef in their smokehouse and muttered, "I sure hope you had the sense to bury the branded hide far and deep, you wife-beating, stock-stealing ass."

He went back into the cabin. The woman on the floor looked dead. But when he put his fingers to her waxen throat he felt a moth-wing flutter and told her, "You can make it if you really try, ma'am. I know there's times when life don't feel worth all the bother. But you got your boy to think of."

To his surprise, she'd heard him. She didn't open her eyes, but her voice, while soft, was steady as she murmured, "Waiting for Little Dan to grow tall enough to make it on his own is all that's kept me going. Now that he's almost as tall as Big Dan I feels I've done my duty. So if it's all the same to you I'd sure like to be on my way to join the heavenly choir now."

He had to keep her fighting. He leaned his Winchester against the free-stone fireplace and hauled out one of her limp hands to hold. "If you go before your son gets back he'll never forgive you for leaving without saying your proper goodbyes. *I'll be* mad at you, too."

She sighed. "You're always mad at me, Dan. Lord

132

knows I've tried, and we loved each other, once. At least, you *told* me you loved me, and I really did love *you*. What happened to us, Dan? What happened that made you start hitting me instead of kissing me like you used to?"

There were times to talk sense and there were times a lady was in no condition to make sense. So he kissed her limp wrist and told her, "I'm sorry, honey. I was wrong to hit you and I'll never do it again, hear?"

There was a little more grit in her delirious voice, as she told him, "You've told me that time and time again, Dan. Lord knows I *want* to believe you, but this time you even hit the *boy*. I thought you loved our only child, even when you'd been at the jug. But this time you hit Little Dan, too, and I don't reckon I mean to forgive you this time. So let go my fool hand and let me fly on over Jordan, hear?"

He insisted, "Hang on. The boy is on his way with a trained nurse, and he *needs* you. We all need you. You got to hang on."

She sighed. "Well, maybe just until Little Dan gets back, then. I would like to kiss my baby one more time afore I heads for heaven. Lord knows, I've served my time in *hell*."

The next time he spoke to her she didn't answer, but he could tell from her more relaxed breathing that she was more asleep than delirious, now. He wet the wool on her brow again and rose, still facing her with his back to the open door. He was sorry he'd done a fool thing like that when a male voice behind him demanded, "What are you doing in here with my woman, stranger?" in a tone midway between a growl and a whimper.

Longarm kept his hands polite as he slowly turned to face a disgusting mess with a twelve-gauge trained on him. The wife-beater was a tall, skinny drink of water dressed in ragged denim, gumboots, and a blood-caked mop of greasy black hair. He could have used either a shave or a regular beard as well. Longarm ignored the shotgun trained on him, and said, "Howdy. My name is Custis Long. I was passing through when your son informed me the lady of the house was feeling poorly. As anyone can see, he told me true. So I've done what I could to make her comfortable until the boy gets back with some medical attention."

The man scowled. "You had no right laying your hands on my woman, and if you've trifled with her honor, well, we both know what a man has to do about a thing like *that*."

Longarm snorted in disgust. "You sure worry a lot about your woman's honor, for a man who just beat her half to death, and we'll see if it was only *half*, when that nurse gets here."

The nester couldn't meet Longarm's knowing eyes. "That was a family argument I don't have to explain to no damn saddle tramp," he muttered. "You can leave, now. I'll take over in here."

Longarm said, "Not hardly. I ain't about to leave an alley cat in *your* tender care, after seeing how you'd treat a wife and mother. As to whether I get to ride on, or have to take you back to town before I do, that will depend on whether she lives or not. Do you want me to take a look at that split scalp of your own whilst we wait? You ain't bleeding fresh, but he surely gave you a good smack with the flat of that old axe, didn't he?"

The man in the doorway raised the muzzle of his twelve-gauge as Longarm took a step toward him. "Don't try nothing. I'll kill you. I mean it," he warned.

Longarm growled, "Aw, shit," grabbed the muzzle in his left hand, and made the man let go the other end with a right cross that sent him flying out the door to land on his rump in the dusty dooryard.

As Longarm tossed the twelve-gauge one way and stepped the other to stomp some sense into the silly son of a bitch, he saw the man he'd downed had rolled up into a ball on one side to whimper and bawl, "Don't hit me again! *Please* don't hit me again! I'm hurt bad. My own son just slew me with an axe and I ain't in no shape to fight right now."

Longarm kicked him in the ribs to shut him up. "Get up and show some grit, you yellow-bellied nothing-much. Look, I'm taking my gun rig off. I'm tossing it aside, so's you can show me what a ferocious he-man you are. Get up and fight a man, instead of women and children, for a change. Don't you want the world to admire how ferocious you are? Ain't that the whole point of all your man-of-the-house heroics?"

Big Dan, as he'd made them call him, stayed right where he was, at Longarm's feet, as he blubbered, "I can't fight *you,* I'm hurt, and you're too big."

Longarm sunk another boot tip into him, spat on him, and said, "You got that backwards. A grown man would be too big for you if you was feeling fine and he was five feet tall. Me or any other grown man could piss on you right now, if I felt like pissing right now, and you'd just enjoy the shower like the shit-eating dog you are. Ain't that right? Ain't you nothing but a whimper-faced woman-striking shit-eating dog?"

The man groveling at his feet didn't answer until Longarm toed him again and made him say it aloud, every word. Then Longarm strode over to recover his gun rig from the grass, strap it back on, and say, "You can get up now. I won't hit you no more, now that we've both agreed on what you are. We'd best have a look at that scalp, and your upper lip's getting a mite fat, too."

He led the man back inside and sat him in a corner on a nail keg. Then he stood over him with the canteen and a dish cloth, saying, "Hold still. I only mean to wash the yard dirt off and let you scab clean. Chicken-dust in a cut can infect nasty as hell."

The slightly injured man whimpered as Longarm tried to clean him up a little. Longarm said, "That scalp could do with a few stitches, but it ain't so bad."

Big Dan said, "My own boy done that to me. Hit his own dear daddy with an axe, he did!"

Longarm said, "Good for him. Had he buried the blade in your thick skull, there ain't a jury in this country as would have found him guilty of anything more than doing right by his own mother. I want you to ponder them words, you dumb bastard. I fear your days as the ferocious ruler of this pathetic roost are numbered. Your boy's growed big enough to fight you back like a man, and we both know woman-beaters ain't up to fighting *men*, don't we?"

The man of the house sobbed, "I never meant to hurt the boy. I never meant to really hurt Blanche, yonder. But she kept nagging me and nagging me, and you've no idea how sharp that little gal's tongue can cut a man when she really gets to work on him about every bitty little mistake he's ever made."

Longarm said, "You're wrong. Show me a man who ain't been fussed at by a woman and I'll show you a deaf monk. That's just the way the Good Lord created the unfair sex. It ain't their fault. It ain't our fault. It's just the way men and women was created. Women get to fuss at us because they ain't big and strong enough to beat us up. We got to take it from 'em because that's just their nature and it just ain't right to beat up anybody smaller, softer, and prettier than you are. Even if they ain't pretty no more."

"But she kept going on and on about how shiftless I am and how poor we've ever been," Big Dan protested.

"I ain't finished. But since you brought it up, I can see as good as any woman that you *are* shiftless and poor. I don't know why you picked such a poor place to homestead any more than she did. But you did, and you're either mighty lazy when you're sober or drunk

136

most of the time. For this spread is a disgrace and you know it. It wouldn't cost you a cent to chink these walls with free mud and straw. A man with the ambition of a robin-bird would have sodded the roof by now, and at least drilled in some turnips and spuds. But let that go. I suspect she'd already told you that much, and more, before you beat her half to death. Let's talk about why men beat women in the first damn place."

The now battered husband stared blankly up at him to say, "I thought we'd just agreed on that."

Longarm shook his head. "Not really. I know of a rich minister in Denver who beat his wife to death for not bringing his pipe and slippers fast enough one night. It's a fact of nature that men and women annoy one another now and again. It's also a fact of nature that *most* men *don't* kick the shit out of their women. They have the manly option of paying them no mind or leaving them. Yelling back don't help, and hitting them is just plain wrong. Ninety-nine out of a hundred men are able to accept them rules of nature. The few like you who can't ain't really beating women. They're beating their own feelings of fear and helpless rage at a world they ain't men enough to stand up to like men."

Big Dan started to protest. Longarm said, "Shut up and listen. I may be saving your life, if your wife lives. For in my line of work I have to study on how folk get in trouble. So I know where hitting gals can take a man."

He paused to reach for a smoke before he said, "Men start out abusing women and children because it makes a weak man feel more strong, at first. A man who's afraid to face a male boss or a bully can still rant and roar about his own house like the cock of the walk, and neither his wife nor his kids is half as likely to back him down as the world all around outside is. But you see, Dan, deep down inside, the domineering cuss has to *know* this. So no matter how much his family cowers from him, it don't give him the full satisfaction he'd get from winning just one fight with another man. He wants to feel brave. He wants to feel respected. So he has to push harder at home. He has to feel he's got his wife and kids scared skinny of him and, even when they are, he has to keep proving it by acting meaner and meaner until, sooner or later, something like what just happened here today just has to happen."

Big Dan started to cry. Longarm said, "Aw, hell, you could at least *try* to act like a grown man," as he turned away in disgust.

That was when he saw the gal staring soberly at him from the open doorway. She was younger and prettier than he'd expected a midwife to be. She wore a blue dress and a matching sunbonnet over her light brown braided hair. She had a black oilcloth medical kit in one hand. He didn't know how long she'd been there or how much she'd heard. He said, "Howdy, ma'am. I didn't hear you ride in. This cuss on the keg ain't hurt bad. I think the lady on the floor, yonder, has a concussion."

The pretty midwife nodded and moved to drop to her knees by the battered wife. As Longarm watched, Little Dan came in from tethering Ramona and her cart horse, out front. He looked awkwardly at his father and stammered, "Howdy, Pappy. I'm sure glad I didn't kill you, after all."

The nester rose, weeping like a baby, to grab his son and hug him, sobbing, "Oh, I'm so sorry, son."

The young midwife looked up at Longarm. "You were right. There's really nothing we can do for her now, but wait and see."

Longarm glanced at the sunslant outside and asked, "How long might that be, ma'am? I'm a lawman, working on another case. I got to get up to Atlantic City as soon as I can."

The young midwife said, "I can't answer that yet. She could come out of it any time between right now or a couple of days. Or she could become another case for the law, any minute."

Longarm nodded grimly and said, "That's why I ain't left yet. I don't know if we're still inside Saint Stephens Township but we are on federal range, homesteaded or not. Nobody but Uncle Sam's land office really owns this land entire until it's been improved and dwelt on, some."

He turned to the nester hugging his kid in the doorway and called out, "How long have you folk been here?"

The boy said, "About two years, come fall."

Longarm sighed and said, "I was afraid of that. If she don't make it, we're talking federal."

Then he said, "If you two gents are through hugging one another, we'd best get back to work. I got some canned food in my saddlebags. But I ain't about to walk all the way to the creek for pot water."

Big Dan said he'd go. Longarm said, "Not hardly. I mean to keep a closer eye than that on you. I'm already chasing one murderer all over Robin Hood's barn, and there are limits to my patience. I want the boy to go for water. You'd best stay here and start chinking them log walls, hear?"

The man looked surprised. "How can you worry about a chore like that at a time like this?"

Longarm answered, "That's easy. I can't see you doing it *without* a grown man here to make you, and any fool can see it needs doing."

Then he excused himself and stepped outside to find that shotgun and empty it as he called, "You can come out and start pulling grass up, now. Make sure you don't pull nothing but grass if you don't want your chinking to fall out. Plantain and dock wilts a lot as it dries."

The nester came out, staring uncertainly at the slopes all around. Longarm said, "I don't care which way you pick. Just so you don't go too far."

The boy came out, toting a cast-iron pot and a wooden bucket. Longarm nodded and said, "That ought to do her, in two trips. Your dad will need at least a couple of pails of water to mix with the grass and mud."

"Is it all right if I help him, mister?" asked the kid.

Longarm shrugged and said, "He's your kin. It's your cabin as needs the chinking." So the son went one way and the father another as Longarm strode over to the midwife's buckboard and told her dapple-gray draft pony, "We'd best unhitch you so's you and old Ramona can graze. Lord knows when any of us will be able to get *out* of here."

As he was leading the gray from between the shafts, the gal who owned it came out, smiled when she saw what he was up to, and said, "Oh, thank you. You must have read my mind. My name is Ann Fletcher, by the way."

He told her it wasn't his fault that his folk had named him Custis and as he led both horses around to the back she stayed in step with him as if she had something else on her mind.

He tethered both brutes on long leads to the corral rail, to let them graze outside it. She said, "I heard what you were telling Dan Hogan about wife-beaters before. I thought *I* was the student of psychology in these parts. But I guess a lawman has to know more than most about such matters as well, eh?"

He shrugged and began to unsaddle Ramona as he said, "It helps some. I wish it helped more. I meet most of the gents I have to arrest some time *after* they should have talked to a head doctor."

She told him he was nevertheless an unusually understanding gent. He got the saddle off, draped it over a corral rail, and rubbed Ramona's back with the saddle blanket before putting that aside to dry as well. As he turned back to her he said, "I don't know if I done these folk any good or not. If she dies I have to take him back into town to stand trial for it. If she don't, he might stop beating her, or he might beat her some more until he kills her, or his son kills him, or whatever. As long as everyone's alive and more or less well when I ride out again, it won't be my unwelcome chore. Do you know how to cook?"

She blinked in surprise, dimpled at him, and said she'd never had any complaints. So he said, "That's good. My cooking don't bother me, or I wouldn't cook that way. But I *have* had complaints. I got some pork and beans, tomato preserves, half a smoked sausage and some real Arbuckle coffee. There ought to be some wild onion higher up, or even mountain cress, if it ain't all dried out. We'll need some padding to feed so many on one rider's iron rations. So I'd best poke about."

She stayed with him as he walked upslope behind the homestead. He didn't mind. She was nice company and, as it turned out, not bad at herbing. From time to time she'd bend over to pluck a weed he wasn't so sure one ought to eat. When he came up with a fistful of bitty wild onion bulbs and mentioned death camus she said, "Those are onions. I have an easy way to keep from eating death camus by mistake. I never eat *any* kind of camus."

He chuckled. "That's a good way to be sure. Even Shoshone have been known to poison themselves that way. But the camus that's safe to eat sure tasted good, one time, when I was left afoot a spell with nothing better to eat."

She asked when that had been. "Never mind," he said. "I don't like to dwell on Indian scouting. I *like* most Indians, when they ain't on the warpath."

She looked away and said, sort of tight-lipped, "I don't. The Shoshone killed my husband two summers ago. Was that the uprising you just spoke of?"

"Yep. I'm sure sorry I shot off my fool mouth about Indians, Miss Ann. I didn't do so to rake up hurtful memories."

"I know. I can tell you don't like to hurt anybody. I must say you sure picked an odd profession for such a kind-hearted man."

He shrugged and said, "It pays better than herding cows, and I don't figure I'm hurting *most* folk. Most folk come decent. By putting away the few bad apples in the barrel, one could say I was sort of helping the majority of the folk I meet."

Then he grinned sheepishly. "There I go, trying to explain my fool self to a lady who reads books about psychology."

She laughed sweetly. "That's what they say we *all* do, about some things. The world could use more men who excuse their actions your way, Custis. I get to see a lot of meanness in my line of work, too, and it's amazing how many spiteful things can be rationalized as one's duty to the Lord and Queen Victoria."

He said he'd noticed that, and added, "As long as I'm picking greens with a lady who knows more than most about sick heads, I got some posers for you to study on with me."

They kept gathering as he filled her in on the homicidal lunatic he'd been chasing when he'd been sidetracked by this lesser case of human error. He noticed she listened well, without missing any bets in the deep grass they were moving through. She let him finish before she said, "Well, I'm only trained to the grade of practical nurse. But it certainly sounds as if that poor boy is suffering from dementia praecox."

"Does that mean he's just plain loco?" he asked, and she said, "About as crazy as one can get and still function. As I understand it, victims of the madness think everyone's against them. So they convince themselves they're somebody more important and powerful, who

142

can deal with enemies better."

He hunkered down to pick a tasty-looking weed as he said, "I already had that part figured. What I'm more worried about is whether Black Jack Junior is really demented or just trying to slicker me."

She flopped down in the grass beside him. He started to ask why and decided that would make him loco, too. He rolled to sit beside her, muttering, "We got more greens than a rabbit could eat for supper."

She lay back on her elbows, her own greens piled where she'd have had a lap if she'd been sitting up straighter, and opined, "I don't see how the killer you're after could be *faking* madness. He'd *have* to be mad to be carrying on the way he's been carrying on, wouldn't he?"

Longarm plucked a grass stem to chew before he explained, "I still get the feeling I've been missing something. The real Black Jack Slade didn't vanish into thin air after he pistol-whipped or gunned somebody. He tended to stick around and brag about it. His young, meaner mimic ain't like that at all. One minute he's there, carrying on even worse than the original, and the next time you look he's just not anywhere. Could that demented whatever make a cuss act *sneaky* as well as ornery?"

She said, "Of course. People with delusions of persecution can act fearsomely cunning, and they often suffer from a split personality as well."

He frowned. "Does that mean he could think he was more than one nut? Say, Wellington and Napoleon at the same time?"

"More like Wellington one time and Napoleon another. I even read of a case in France where this real French peace officer spent half his time as a master criminal and the rest of the time as the detective assigned to the case. It appears he made a sincere effort as a detective to track his own criminal side down."

Longarm chuckled at the picture. "Did he ever catch himself?" he asked.

She shook her sunbonnet and said, "Not exactly. He was caught by other French detectives when his criminal personality walked into the trap his detective personality had set up. The point is that both his personalities were *sincere*. He wasn't putting on an act when he was either."

Longarm sighed. "I sure wish the timid little Joseph Slade would offer some suggestions on how to catch his blacker side. But if he does turn into a milk-toast, between such moments, he ain't seen fit to turn his other self in. I got another poser for you, Miss Ann. I've been taking him at his word he thinks he's that long-dead gunslick, and trailing him as if he was real. So far, aside from the way he behaved in Denver when he was just starting to act crazy, he's done all his dirty deeds on or about the old stomping grounds of his idol, former self, or whatever. Do I sound loco, too, in assuming he just has to stay close to the old Overland Trail?"

She told him, "I think you've been unusually wise, for a peace officer without a degree in lunacy. The fact that the poor boy headed north to the Overland Trail proves he's acting under some compulsion."

"Yeah, he could shoot folk just as good where he was, if that's all he wanted to do. I just wish he'd stay compulsed more *visible* along the Overland Trail. But whether he tries to ride through the South Pass up ahead dressed in goat-hair chaps or as a Baptist minister, I'll have him. Folk of any description come few and far between in trail towns like Atlantic City, and he'll have to stop for water there, after riding dry a good stretch above the headwater slopes. I just have to watch for any stranger that small and—"

"Have you considered him riding sidesaddle, in skirts?" she cut in.

He started to tell her that was silly until he took her suggestion. "Thunderation! That works! Even *he* must have noticed by now how short and small he is. Even in his wild cow duds he ain't no bigger than you are, and it stands to reason a lunatic could think he was Josephine as well as Napoleon. He come home from the army to an older sister who could be missing at least one dress. I never asked, and she might not have noticed in any case."

He thought about the way the killer had vanished so quickly with posse riders hot on his tail and grabbed her to give her a big kiss as he told her, "You're smart as hell, Lord love you. Oh, sorry, ma'am. I wasn't trying to be forward."

She smiled up at him from under her sunbonnet and told him she wasn't sore. He let her drop back in the grass as he sat up in it and stared down the slope at the shabby homestead, growling, "Your fine suggestion makes up for the day I just lost on more serious business. But I'm still sorry I ever saw that fool kid running for you."

She said, *"I'm* not. I mean, if you hadn't wrapped her up so well before I could get there, she'd surely have died before the boy and me arrived."

He shrugged. "That's why I wrapped her. And now I'm stuck here until we see how it turns out. How do *you* figure her chances, Miss Ann?"

She said, "Fifty-fifty. I can't get her to take liquids, and in this thin, dry mountain air she needs them more than she might in moister and thicker air. I've seen concussion victims wake up bright-eyed and bushy-tailed, and I've seen them just pass away without *ever* waking. I wish we had some way of peeking inside her skull without cutting it open. But we don't. I guess we'll always have to just *guess* about brain injuries."

He didn't answer. Women couldn't stand a man who

didn't babble every stray thought, so she asked, "Will you have to arrest Dan Hogan if she doesn't make it?"

He favored her with a raised eyebrow. "Did you think I was sticking around to pin a medal on him? The reason gents in my line of work hate these domestic cases is that, should she wake up with him holding her hand and telling her how sorry he is, she'll never in this world press charges, and I'll have wasted all this time."

"And if she dies?"

"He's mine to keep and cherish. As the only law in sight, it'll be my duty to arrest him, of course. A lady can't forgive even a husband for killing her *entire*."

She sighed. "Lord knows I have little sympathy for any wife-beater. But poor Dan Hogan isn't all bad. You were so right when I heard you telling him what made him act that way. I've known them since they came out here to try homesteading. The poor man tried, at first. But he just didn't have what it takes to make a go of it in such unforgiving country. It's not his fault he's a failure. What do you think they'll do to him?"

She blanched when Longarm said flatly, "They'll hang him high. It ain't *their* fault he's a failure, neither, and in such a thin-settled county there won't be a man on the jury who won't have heard he's a man who beats his woman, and like as not steals beef."

She insisted, "That hardly seems just. At worse he could only be found guilty of manslaughter, not premeditated murder, right?"

He shrugged. "Jerkwater juries don't worry much about the finer points of the law. If she dies, he'll be lucky if they even go through the formalities. Wyoming is still a territory, and such local law as there may be is still sort of ad hoc. I don't like it all that much, either. But if she dies, all I can do is hand him over to the nearest sheriff. After that it'll be out of my hands."

She didn't look as relaxed, now. She said, "Well, I'll

just have to make sure she lives, then," and got to her feet to sort of flounce down the slope ahead of him, not looking back, as he muttered, "I'll never figure their kind, Lord. That makes another woman mad at me for just doing my duty, damn it."

Chapter 12

At Ann's suggestion, they'd supped late to take some edge off the long hours of waiting ahead. She had cooked a fair supper from the wild greens and smoked beef out back, saving Longarm's iron rations for him, after all, except for the coffee. She made the coffee strong so she could stay awake and watch for a change in the condition of the battered wife in Longarm's bedroll.

It was crowded and stinky enough in the cabin with the walls fresh-chinked with wet mud and the softwood fire reeking of sap and pitch. Longarm stepped out to sit on the front steps and blow smoke rings at the setting sun. Ann came out a little later to sit beside him and murmur, "No change. I can't tell whether she's sleeping sound or dying, and poor Dan Hogan is beside himself with worry and remorse."

"He ought to be", Longarm said. "It's the boy I feel more sorry for. Having a daddy hanged is a hard thing to live down."

"I know. It would be kinder if you just shot Big Dan. But I can't let you do that, either," she told him.

He didn't want to know how she aimed to stop him from making the arrest he'd have to if the woman died. "Our two ponies have had plenty of juicy grass and forbs, out back. But I still ought to water 'em as darkness falls. Leading a horse to water is easier than toting water to a horse. So I guess I'll lead 'em down to the creek. Do you want to come along?"

She said, "I'd love to. I'm tired of just sitting about waiting for poor Blanche to go one way or the other. But the creek's a mite far. I'd best stay closer to my patient lest she go into convulsions, as they sometimes do."

He nodded, rose, and walked around the cabin to untether the stock and lead them away for some roaming in the gloaming. The creek was less than half a mile off, but it was still getting dark by the time he'd decided they'd had enough and hauled them back out of the running water. They didn't want to come back to the spread with him, so they were having some discussion about their future plans when, as Longarm was tugging and cussing, he heard running and yelling and turned his head to see what could only be Little Dan Hogan tear-assing off down the creek again, as if he'd decided to make a habit of that.

Longarm called after him. The boy didn't answer. He just vanished into the darkness toward town. Hoping he was guessing wrong about the reason, Longarm mounted Ramona bareback and, leading the dapple gray, got back up to the cabin as fast as he could.

As he dismounted out front the young midwife popped out to say simply, "She's gone."

When Longarm forgot himself in front of a lady to mutter, "Aw, shit!" Ann said, "You can say that again."

He followed her inside, where Big Dan Hogan was hunkered over his dead wife, bawling like a baby, and told the girl, "Right. You're going to have to help. Hitch your gray to your buckboard whilst I get the two of 'em out front and saddle my own mount."

"Can't you wait even a split second to turn that poor brute over to the hangman?" she snapped. "Don't argue, woman," he said. "Split seconds is all we got to work with. That kid was running like a deer to tell the whole infernal community his mother had been beat to death by his father. Move. I'll take care of what's in here."

She picked up her black bag and ducked out the door. Longarm stepped over to the sobbing husband and put a not-unkind hand on his shoulder to shake it as he said, "We got to pick her up, my bedding and all, and carry her out to the buckboard, Dan. If you ain't up to helping, stay out of my way, and I can manage."

The bawling man couldn't even make sense, let alone help. Longarm shoved him aside and bent to pick up his dead wife's pathetic remains. "May as well leave the lamp lit. They'd only light it some more when they ride in. Follow me, in the name of the law, Dan Hogan."

The sobbing man did, protesting that he'd only meant to make his woman stop fussing at him. Longarm didn't answer. Outside, he saw that the young midwife had already hitched her cart horse between the shafts. He'd figured she'd know how, since she owned the rig. He carried the corpse over and put it behind the spring seat on the flat hickory bed. Then he made Dan Hogan climb aboard as well and reached for the set of handcuffs he carried on the back of his gun rig. He cuffed Hogan's right wrist to the left leaf spring under the seat and told him, "You can brace your shoulders against the back of Miss Ann's seat. Your skinny behind may take more of a beating from the bed, but you deserve a good spanking in any case. Make sure your wife don't bounce off, hear?"

He turned to see that the owner of the buckboard was

standing there staring at him. "Get aboard, damn it. Do you know the way to the railroad stop at Lander?" he asked.

"Of course. It's the county seat. But it's so *far*, Custis. It's must be forty miles or more," she protested.

He said, "I hope that's far enough. Get in and start driving. I'll fetch my saddle and catch up with you. What are you waiting for, woman? It was *your* notion to charge this dumb brute with manslaughter rather than murder. I don't *like* him that much. So move it on out before we have company that's sure to hate him worse than *I* do!"

She gulped, took her buggy whip from its socket, and they were off and running. Longarm ran, too, back to the corral to get his saddle. The sounds of her wagon wheels had faded away by the time he had everything he owned except some blankets he no longer wanted secured to old Ramona. He forked a long leg into the saddle and said adios to the tedious surroundings that had cut his lead on Black Jack Junior a whole damned day.

When Ann heard the sound of his following hoof-beats as she was topping a distant rise, she reined to a stop to wait for him. As he joined her he said, "Keep going. At a trot. We got too many miles to cover if we run 'em. Do you reckon that gray is good for forty miles, non-stop?"

She said of course not and he said, "They won't think to follow wagon wheels and hoofmarks before they've studied on it some. They'll be trying to cut the trail of our only living passenger, and those who know him know he don't keep a mount."

Both she and the man cuffed behind her tried to ask what he was talking about at the same time. "Shut up, Dan Hogan," he said. "You're nothing but a favor to less disgusting folk, even if you had the brains to understand." Then he told the woman, "There's no Wyoming court that wouldn't hang him, manslaughter or no. They hang you for horse theft under *local* custom. But I'm a federal deputy and there's a federal court at the county seat of Lander. Federal law takes a less draconian view on anything less than murder in the first degree. So I mean to turn him in to the U.S. government in Lander and point out that he never had the brains to premeditate anything."

She gasped and said, "Oh, you darling man!" Even the prisoner behind her perked up, until she asked how much time they'd likely let him off with.

Longarm said, "Twenty at hard, if he's lucky. That still saves Little Dan from having to say he saw his daddy do the rope dance, when future friends and possible in-laws ask. It ain't half as awkward to just say kin is . . . ah . . . away."

She nodded and said she'd see that the lad was taken in by decent folk, later. "That shouldn't be hard. The boy's nigh full grown, and I noticed that, even reformed, his dear old dad didn't work half as hard at fixing up the cabin back there."

"Can the boy still claim it as his own?" she asked.

"Nope. It'll revert to the land-office as an unproven claim. But nobody with a lick of sense would have tried to nest in mountain cow country without no cows, in any case. Given a few years as an honest young cowhand, Little Dan ought to be able to buy a way better spread on his own. It was with hopes I might be able to keep him honest that I undertook this mad adventure. Lord knows how much more of a lead I'm giving that infernal killer I'm *supposed* to be looking for."

She shot him an arch look in the moonlight and said, "Fess up. You can't fool me, Custis Long. Under all that gruffness you're just a nice gent, aren't you?"

"Damn fool is the term you are searching for. And

I'll get even gruffer if that other killer kills again whilst I'm wasting the taxpayers' time on this killer who's only half serious about it."

The prisoner protested again that he'd never meant to kill anybody, let alone his beloved Blanche. Longarm told him he shouldn't have hit her so hard, in that case, and added that he didn't want to hear about it any more. "Save your tears for the federal judge. Let's take this downgrade ahead a mite faster, Miss Ann. For if that posse catches up with us, they might just hang all *four* of us in the enthusiasm of the moment."

They rested and watered their stock every hour or so, but just the same it was getting harder to make them keep going by sunrise, and they were only a little better than halfway. Longarm stared morosely at the trail ahead as they reined in for a breather and told Ann, "You look like you've been dragged through the keyhole backwards, too. We're going to have to camp a spell."

He pointed at the open and gentle slope off the trail to their east. "Drive over to them pines up the slope. I filled my canteens back at the homestead, and camping any closer to a trailside stream invites all sorts of casual company for breakfast."

She waited until they were almost a quarter of a mile off the wagon trace before she called out, "Wouldn't it make sense to go on into the trees, Custis?"

"Not hardly. Anyone coming along now is sure to see where we turned off through this dew-covered grazing. If they see us, camped at a modest distance for talking to, they might ride on by. If they wonder why we seem to be hiding in the trees, they might not. Anywhere along about here will do as well."

She stopped and he reined in. Both ponies lowered their heads to inhale some dew-wet mountain meadow. Longarm dismounted and helped her unhitch her gray before he unsaddled Ramona and put them on their grazing leads. They were only a few yards from the tree-line. Longarm said, "This grass will be dry enough to sit on by the time we all take a stroll in the woods and bust out the iron rations after all. I see no need to build a fire."

She didn't answer. She was heading for the trees. Neither he nor Big Dan Hogan asked why.

Longarm moved around to unfasten the one cuff from the wagon spring as he told his prisoner, "You can hold it till she gets back. Then we'll *both* go take a leak."

The prisoner didn't answer. He was staring at the body of his dead wife. Longarm had put her aboard with her face covered, but the bouncing had moved the tarp out of the way, some. Longarm covered her waxen face again and said quietly, "She won't spoil too bad in this mountain air before we get her to Lander."

Hogan gagged and said, "She looks so . . . so *dead*."

Longarm moved to steady him as they got his feet to the ground, saying, "Don't go crying about it again. You must have cried a gallon or more by now, and not a single tear made up for any of the tears you made that poor gal shed."

"Don't you think I know that?" Hogan sobbed. "I don't care if they hang me, now. I deserves to be hanged more than once for the way I treated that poor little gal."

The other, more lively gal they were traveling with came out of the trees about then, staring down at the grass as if she was looking for something. Longarm told his prisoner, "Our turn. This way," and led him out of Ann's path, up into the same woods.

When they'd both watered the pines Longarm stared thoughtfully about and decided, "I reckon I'd best cuff you to a stout branch and leave you here for now. We'll pick a low one so's you can stretch out on the pine needles if you want. I'll bring you some grub and water."

The prisoner asked why. Longarm just cuffed him to a low-grown limb and left him to figure it out. He was more polite when Ann asked him, back at the buckboard. He said, "If he ain't with us, when anybody asks, we won't be fibbing when we say he ain't with us, see?"

She told him he was smart again. He stood by the buckboard, opening cans on the tailboard with his pocket knife, as she got her own tarp from under the seat and spread it on the grass nearby. He mixed the contents like a barkeep until he had three cans filled with the same concoction of cold canned beans and tomato preserves. He excused himself a moment and took the prisoner's rations to him in the woods. He handed the can to Hogan and said, "This may hold you. You don't need water with such slop. If you hear loud voices from back here, don't call out to 'em. Miss Ann and me hardly ever yell. Savvy?"

Hogan had had time to guess the plan. He said he meant to stay quiet as a church mouse. Longarm told him that might not be quiet enough and went back to join Ann on her tarp.

It didn't take long to polish off their own slop. Rank having its privileges, they got to wash theirs down with water and a dash of Maryland rye Longarm carried in a saddlebag for snakebite and such social occasions. She asked for more and, after she'd had it, said, "It's funny. I've been up all night and I'm bone-tired, but I don't think I could go to sleep right now if I was back home in my bed."

He resisted the temptation to tell her he wished they were both back home in her bed, and settled for, "It's the tension one feels at times like these. I've gone three or four days and nights without sleep on a serious case, not even trying. I reckon it's like that Professor Darwin says. We're all descended from keen hunters because, before we got civilized enough to live softer, folk who couldn't keep up when times got tense never got to *have* descendants."

"My, you *do* read a lot. Anyone can see you're a keen hunter, as well. But you look sort of . . . well, *confused,* now, Custis. I mean, I can see it, deep in your eyes, that your thoughts are running around inside so fast they seem to be bumping into one another."

He smiled thinly. "Remind me never to play poker with you. You're all too right. It ain't my thoughts bumping noses. I know what's going on. It's conflicting *duties* that are giving me such a bother. Life would be easier on a lawman if it let him just hunt one rascal at a time. But I'm sworn to uphold the law no matter *how* many fools I see breaking it. So I got to run that wife-killer in and, at the same time, I feel like a fool fox-hound who's been sidetracked by a rabbit."

She sighed. "I understand. You're doing this for *me,* aren't you?"

He knew she'd like him better if he said that was it, but he replied, "Not entire, no offense. It is my sworn duty to see justice done, and that poor brute don't figure to get much justice off a jury of his neighbors. He ain't got no friends. I know he'll be treated fair by the federal district court in Lander. So we got to get him there, and we will. Meantime, it's out of my way, and I know I'm losing my lead on that more *serious* killer. What you may see running around behind my eyes is that I know I could be making two awful mistakes at once by trying to do my job two ways at the same time."

She dimpled and said, "Oh, heck, I thought it was because I let you kiss me that other time."

Her sunbonnet hardly got in the way at all. But she still untied it and let it fall off as he kissed her again, harder. For, while he was somewhat confused about his duty to the law, Longarm knew his duty when it was spelled out for him by dimples and big blue eyes.

They wrestled friendly on the tarp for a spell and she

didn't fuss when he ran his free hand over her from the waist up. But when he got his hand under her skirt, kissing her as warmly as they both seemed to feel, she protested in a stifled voice, "Stop that this instant!" So he did.

She sat up, red-faced, and didn't look at him as she added, "I meant out here under the open sky, in front of God and everyone."

He started to ask who could see them, surrounded as they were by such tall grass. But by then he'd sat up, too. So he had to mutter, "Oh, Lord, I've seldom met a gal who was right so often, but when you're right you sure are *right!*"

They could both see the dozen-odd riders headed their way up the slope, riding sort of spread out and wary. Longarm told her, "Stay put and just follow my lead," before he got to his feet and waved a howdy with his hat.

That brought them closer, faster. As he spied the tin star one rider in the lead was wearing Longarm called out, "I reckon I know who you boys are after. I sure hope it ain't me."

The county deputy reined in to stare poker-faced down at Longarm and the girl he could now see behind him. He said, "The boy told us about you two, when he run in to say his father had beat his mother to death. We know who done it. Would you mind telling us how come you rid this way instead of coming into town? When we got to the cabin, even the body was missing."

Longarm knew better than to fib about the bundle they were all staring at, now. He said, "That's easy. I'm law, too. Federal. The Hogan woman was killed on federal land. That's her, on the buckboard. We figured to take her up to the federal court at Lander."

The older star-sporting gent staring hard from his saddle said, "You figured wrong. Blanche Hogan was murdered in Fremont County, and the county wants both her and the skunk as murdered her. In case you're wondering, I'm Fremont County."

Longarm said, "I never said you was from anywhere else. As you can see, we don't have her husband with us. So let's not act greedy. You boys look all you like for *him* and, meanwhile, we'll just carry *her* on up to Lander."

The older lawman in charge of such disgusting odds shook his head. "We're holding the trial in Saint Stephens, and that's where we mean to take the corpse, see?"

"Not hardly. You don't seem to have anyone to try, and you surely don't want a lady turning funny colors in your witness box," Longarm told him.

"We has to prove she's *dead*, don't we?"

"Well, sure you do. But anyone can see she *is*, damn it."

The old-timer knew his law, too. He stared hard at Longarm and said, "You ain't fooling us. We know you mean to hand the coprse in to the federal marshal in Lander so's you feds can steal our case from us."

Longarm grinned knowingly. "Hell, that's only fair. I seen her dead first. I'll tell you what. I'll drop the body off at Lander, and after you boys bring Dan Hogan up to the county seat, we can let the federal and county judges argue about it."

He detected the look of low cunning he'd been trying to inspire in that mean old face and quickly added, innocently, "You mean to bring Hogan up to the county seat for a proper trial as soon as you can catch him, don't you?"

The posse leader was grinning like a polecat regarding the open door of a henhouse. "Why, *sure* we are, old son. Meanwhile, we'll just carry that dead little lady back with us to put on ice until we catch the rascal."

Longarm sighed, turned to Ann, and said, "You'd best move over yonder, out of our line of fire, Miss

Ann. For I do believe my message ain't getting through to these gents."

The older lawman looked more surprised than worried. "I reckon the lady better, too. I hope you've noticed you are making your brag with no more than six rounds against fourteen of us, each packing considerably more ammunition than that?"

Longarm nodded soberly. "What can I tell you? I have to uphold federal law as I see it. The woman was killed under my jurisdiction. I mean to carry her body to Lander as federal evidence. Anyone else who'd like to accompany her in the same condition is free to do so. But I can't promise a tarp for each and every body. It's your move. I've said all I mean to about the matter."

A million years went by. Then one of them muttered, "The kid said he was the one called *Longarm*, Jim."

Old Jim stared hard some more before he shrugged and said, "It must be. Nobody else would act so loco over a durned old dead woman. Let's go, boys. We can still string that rascal up, if we can get to him first."

As they turned to ride off, Longarm took his first deep breath in some time. Ann ran to him, long brown hair streaming, and wrapped her arms around him, sobbing, "Oh, Lord, you were ever so brave and I was ever so scared, Custis! You must be the bravest man who ever lived. I couldn't *believe* it when I saw you stand up to all those horrid men!"

He patted her back. "I couldn't believe it either. I don't know what comes over me at such times. But it goes with my job. I'd say it's safe to sit down some more, now. Where was we when we was so rudely interrupted?"

As they sank back down into each other's arms, she giggled and took his hand to show him. But though he wound up with more than his hand down there, she said they'd have to wait until they got to town before she'd take off *all* her duds and go to town entire with him.

Chapter 13

By the time they got to the county seat and end of the railroad line, the hard way, it was too late in the evening to do much more than ask an undertaker to put Blanche Hogan on ice and ask the turnkey at the federal lockup to hold her husband for the judge, come morning.

Longarm knew he'd lost two whole days of his lead on Black Jack Junior. He stood to lose most of another if the judge turned out to be picky about paperwork. But he was sort of looking forward to the night ahead after all the hours he and poor little Ann had spent prim and proper after that hasty ice-breaking with their fool duds on. So he sprang for the honeymoon suite at the best hotel in town, which wasn't as grand as it might have sounded, and they were so delighted to hire the rooms that they saw no need to ask who she might be when he signed the book for them, singular case.

Once they were upstairs and she was blushing and flustering about checking into a hotel with a man she wasn't even engaged to, he told her, "Hold the thought a spell. I aim to make you feel even more wicked as soon as I can. But I've got some errands to run before this dinky town closes down entire. I got to send me a mess of wires, and I might save time in the morning by picking up the makings of a new bedroll now."

She didn't ask why he wanted a new bedroll. She'd helped him unload the cadaver, still wrapped in his old bedding.

Down on the street, he found the outfitting store had just closed. But the card hanging behind the glass said they opened early in the morning. He made a mental note of the time they'd be open for business and headed next for the Western Union office near the end of the tracks.

Inside, he penciled a message for Billy Vail, bringing him up to date and assuring the home office he hadn't run away with any circus. He figured he still had a lead on the lunatic he hoped to bottleneck on the divide to the west. But it wasn't nearly as long a lead as before. So he wrote out a detailed warning, tossing in the suggestion that the want could be disguised as a normal man or even a woman, and carried both forms to the counter.

The telegraph clerk in Lander was around fifty, making him an old-timer in a rapidly changing West, so he felt free to scan the messages and opine, "You don't want to send this one to South Pass City. The Overland stages crossed the divide by way of *Bridger's* Pass, not the one that colored gent found."

Longarm frowned. "Are you sure we ain't talking about the Wells, Fargo stages?" he asked. "I confess the railroad put all the transcontinental stagecoaches out of business before I ever got to ride coast-to-coast so uncomfortable. But I was told the Overland Trail ran through South Pass."

The older man shook his head and insisted, "Bridger's. I ain't saying Overland never sent a *freight*

162

wagon over the South Pass now and again. But time was money to a mail coach. So most used Bridger's route, and to hell with the grade."

Longarm swore softly. "Send that same message to every law office in the great divide basin, then. For Lord only knows where a gent mapping out the Overland Trail from London, England, might have told a homicidal maniac it ran."

Western Union agreed and, having covered all bets, Longarm went across to a trackside saloon to consult expert opinion on just where in a lot of square miles he might be able to set up his ambush.

The cow and railroad hands he found enjoying their quitting-time cheer in the rinkydink saloon were more than willing to help out a man they considered to be a poor wayfaring stranger lost in their mountains. They did their best, calling one another fools if not greenhorns, as Longarm gained a grudging respect for the gents trying to write even a penny dreadful based on fact or fable out this way.

Folk had to be self-confident, independent thinkers to come west in the first place. Like many poorly educated gents who'd had to learn a lot, sudden, old-timers who'd survived any time at all tended to be know-it-alls who just couldn't admit they might be guessing. Ten years was a long time in country that had changed so much, so fast, and since the Overland Trail had been licked by the railroad that far back, Longarm suspected at least half the opinionated rascals had never even *seen* the mail coaches they claimed to know so much about. One old whiskey drummer who said he traveled all over creation, swore on his dear mother's honor that he'd ridden the Overland stage over Bridger's Pass more than once. But he'd also ridden the Butterfield stage through Apache Pass with the famous Deadwood Dick driving. The old drummer confided, "Deadwood Dick is really a colored man, like they say Sublette was. But that boy sure could drive. You should have seen us going lickety-split with them Apache chasing us for miles. I helped, of course. The shotgun messenger got arrowed. So I had to climb up aside Deadwood Dick as he was holding the traces with his teeth and popping off Apache left and right with his big old Pattersons."

A younger cowhand, who wasn't old enough to tell tales like that without getting called on them, told Longarm he distinctly recalled the Overland coaches passing by his home spread down by Bitter Creek when he was just a lad of six or seven. Longarm thanked him gravely for the information. He was too polite to point out that the railroad town of Bitter Creek couldn't have been there earlier than Sixty-eight or -nine, or that when his informant could have been six or seven the Shoshone still owned that part of the world.

He went back to the hotel to find Ann already undressed and under the covers. He told her not to look so hurt, because he'd only had two beers in the line of duty.

She forgave him, and then some, once he'd shucked his own duds and climbed in with her. She blushed all over when he tossed the covers away to do it right, with a pillow shoved under her pretty little rump. As he got atop her she protested, "You could have at least trimmed the lamp, you wicked boy! We're both stark naked and I feel sure it can't be proper to watch what we're doing and . . . Oh, watch what you're doing! It's too deep this way, and I feel so embarrassed in this position with the lamp lit and, and, yesssss! That feels so marvelous, even if it does look just awful!"

He didn't think she looked awful at all. He'd thought he'd gotten to know her soft sweet body, even though a lot of textile had been in his line of vision. But her thin summer dress hadn't followed half as many delightful curves as she'd been hiding under them. She was in fine shape because of honest work, with just enough female larding under her soft, smooth skin to keep her from looking muscular.

Later, when he finally trimmed the lamp and they were cuddled up like old pals under the top sheet, she nuzzled her pert nose against his collar bone and confessed, "I've always wondered what it would feel like to do it right out and natural, like a whore."

He patted her bare shoulder. "Whores don't do it natural. What *we* just done was natural, not nasty or wicked. Just the way natural folk was made to do it. What sense would there have been for the Lord to make us look so nice to one another in our birthday duds if He hadn't intended us ever to peek?"

She giggled and confided, "In my rounds as a midwife I've heard other women confess to worse than fornicating with the lamp lit."

He said, "We'd best try for some sleep. We've had a long day, with no sleep the night before, and come morning the judge's sure to make us fill out fine-print depositions about the Hogan case."

She brightened. "Oh, do you think we'll get to bear witness at Dan's trial?"

"I don't see why," he said. "Neither of us ever saw him beat her, and they'll have his confession as well as the boy's testimony."

She said, "Oh," in a small hurt voice.

He didn't have to ask her why. "I'd like to spend a month or more in this bed with you, honey," he said. "But I told you in the beginning I was trailing that killer and though it pains me, too, I just have to move on, come morning."

She snuggled closer, sighed, and said, "I know. I'd have never let you have it so soon if I'd thought you might stick around long enough for a proper romance. Do you reckon we'll ever get a chance to be like this together again, darling?"

He said he didn't know. She heaved a defeated sigh

165

and said, "I doubt it, too. So this is another situation I've often wondered about. I get to read a lot, living alone, since the Shoshone caught my man alone in the hills. I've always wondered what it would be like to spend just one night of love with a handsome stranger."

He rolled on his side to run his hand down her soft belly as he told her, "I wouldn't want a friend to feel frustrated." But, as he proceeded to finger her friendly, she said, "Wait. Knowing this may be the last time I'll meet such an understanding gent, I've been thinking of a book I have among my medical texts. It ain't sold to the general public. It's put out as a warning about how folk get to acting when they go sex-mad, and I suspect that's what's just happened to me."

"You're more likely just curious. A warm-natured gal who'd never done it with all her duds off would have a right to be. But I'm game for anything that doesn't hurt."

She began to fondle him back as she shyly confessed, "I could never do half those awful things. But there's this one illustration . . . Lord knows how they ever got anyone to pose in such a position."

She made him relight the lamp and adjust the mirror on the dresser as well. And it did calm her down enough for Longarm to get a little sleep, at last.

The day started out just fine. They made love by the dawn's early light, and enjoyed a hearty breakfast to restore their strength before they went to see how long the judge meant to keep them in town.

That was where things started to go wrong, for Longarm, at least. Ann didn't look as upset when the crusty old district judge told them that while he meant to offer Dan Hogan a fair and speedy trial, he expected them to appear as witnesses.

Longarm protested, "I never saw the fool kill his woman, Your Honor, and, hell, he's confessed he beat her to death, and I got more important places to be!"

The judge said, "If you cuss again I'll have to hold you in contempt of court, Deputy. I know you're more used to the big city and its hasty ways. I know you feel I'm just a glorified J.P. in a one-horse town. But let me tell you, son, we do things right in *this* man's court of justice!"

"Then let me go on after that more ominous killer," said Longarm. "You don't need my testimony, even if I could swear I saw the man beat his women. His boy did, and he's owned up to it."

The stubborn old judge shook his head. "The boy is a minor. His testimony counts, but not as much as that of a grown man or even a woman, no offense, Miss Ann. The accused is an adult, sort of, but should he retract his confession in open court we'll need the two of you to back the prosecution's word that he confessed to both of you as well."

Longarm groaned. "I know full well how often a gent facing hard time considers telling it another way after he's had some words with a slick defense lawyer, Your Honor. But you still have this lady and the boy, and I can leave a sworn deposition for the court, can't I?"

"Nope. As a known peace officer with a good rep, who heard the words of both the dying woman and the man who killed her, your testimony will carry the most weight. If you won't stay willing for the trial I'll just have to hold you in another cell as a material witness. So what's it going to be?"

Longarm shot a look at the blushing Ann and decided, "I'd as soon stay willing, at the hotel. But how much time are we talking about, Your Honor?"

The judge thought before he said, "Oh, we can start the trial as soon as we get the boy up here by rail. Let's say day after tomorrow, to be safe. The trial shouldn't take more than two or three days if he decides to make a fight of it. Way less than that if he don't go back on his confession. So, all in all, you should be able to go on after that outlaw by the end of the week."

Longarm took a deep breath and tried to keep from snarling as he said, "Your Honor, by that time my want may have made it over the mountains to Lord knows where."

But the judge insisted, "Joseph Slade is not the one being tried by this district court. Dan Hogan is. So, like the Indian chief said, I have spoken."

He meant it. By that afternoon Longarm had gotten Billy Vail and even the judge of the Denver District Court to wire that the mule-headed cuss in Lander was obstructing justice. But he wouldn't budge. So, while the next few nights were delightful, the days wore on tedious as hell.

Longarm spent a lot of time at the Western Union, trying to trap that other killer by wire if they wouldn't let him chase after him personal. It was sort of surprising how much a lawman could learn that way, even when he couldn't *do* anything. Longarm began to suspect that once they had those new Bell telephones strung everywhere, he as well as the men he got to chase figured to be out of business. Even having to wait for answers, he was able to establish that he might not have caught the rascal even had he been allowed to follow his original plan. For tiny town after town in the high country to the west reported back that, no, they hadn't spied any strangers of any description trying to get over the mountains by any trail, in open country, where a rider on a rise could see for miles in all directions.

By the afternoon the judge finally got around to throwing twenty years for manslaughter at the weeping Dan Hogan, it was too late for serious riding, even had Longarm known where to ride, now. So he took Ann and a bottle of rye to bed at the hotel early. As they were making love she suddenly blurted, "It's over between us, isn't it, darling?"

He kissed her. "Not until the cruel gray dawn. I'm sorry if I seem distracted tonight, honey. It ain't you. It's that loco little Black Jack Junior. I think I've lost him for good."

They knew one another well enough to talk and make love at the same time. So she hugged him reassuringly with her thighs and said, "I'm sure you'll pick up his trail when he acts crazy some more, dear."

He shook his head. "I was supposed to catch him *before* he killed again, not follow a dotted line of victims as I was wasting time up here. In that courtroom, I mean. *This* part has been mighty fine."

She thanked him with a teasing twist of her torso and said, "He may be in remission, you know."

"I didn't know. What are you talking about?" he said.

"Sometimes victims of dementia praecox just stop. They don't get better. There's no treatment for that condition. But a split personality can split again, to somebody crazy in yet *another* way, see?"

He grimaced. "Oh, swell. I could be chasing a Black Jack Slade Junior who thinks he's Buffalo Bill?"

She said, "I'm trained as a midwife, not a head doctor. But I do recall reading that the condition tends to get worse, not better. If he's still alive, sooner or later, something is sure to rub him the wrong way again and, when you rub dementia praecox the wrong way it goes off like dynamite."

"I've noticed that about the little rascal. He may think he's someone else, now. But I'd have heard if he'd been killed, acting crazy or any other way. I even found out how his model wound up buried in Salt Lake so mysterious."

"Does it really matter?" she asked, moving her hips faster. He decided it didn't, just then. But later, as they were cuddled calmer, he said, "It was neither a geographical mistake by an English writer nor that notion

169

another had that his wife was a Mormon. They just put his box on the wrong train. When it got to Salt Lake City, late in July, old Jack was so stinky that they didn't want to ship him *half* way back to Illinois. So the railroad sprang for a handsome marker on hallowed ground, and his kin agreed not to sue them after all."

She didn't sound interested. She snuggled closer and said, "I wish *both* of them were dead and buried, so you wouldn't have to leave in the morning. Oh, Custis, so *soon?*"

He kissed her again and said, "I ain't kissing you because I'm horny. I'm kissing you because you just gave me a grand notion."

Chapter 14

Billy Vail gave Longarm more like general hell when he showed up in Denver at last, empty-handed. Vail said, "Longarm, it has been established that we can't win 'em all. But I've never seen you give up so *soon*. You didn't even go to Montana or Utah after the cuss, and we agreed he was heading for one or the other on the old Overland Trail."

"The trail only goes to Salt Lake, not Virginia City", Longarm said, "and young Slade never meant to go to neither. We just got slickered by a slick and cunning killer, not a lunatic. Do you want to tag along and share the credit for the arrest?"

"Sure, if you can prove Joseph Slade is here in Denver. Can you?" Vail asked.

"Not a hundred percent, before I *find* him. But I expect to before this day is over. Coming, boss?"

Vail glanced out the window before he said, "It's too hot out to chase a hunch. But I'll listen to your hunch. Where do you mean to start?"

"The Banes house, where the killing all started. It ain't far. I may need you, if them army gents are still sore at me."

Vail shook his head. "They ain't. They gave up on the stakeout right after they got word Slade had shot up Fort Halleck, up north. As for that stupid Colonel Walthers, I used the arrest warrant he swore out on you to prove how stupid he was to an old drinking pal in the War Department. So he won't bother you no more if he wants to keep his oak leaves. There's nobody over at the Banes house right now but the killer's elder sister."

Longarm said, "I'd best have a word with her, then," and left alone.

Billy had been right about the heat outside. Longarm was sorry he'd had to change back into his tobacco-brown tweeds and shoestring tie as he walked even that far with the noonday sun beating down on him.

When he got to the house, and Flora Banes née Slade came to her door, he could tell from the feather duster in one hand and the thin poplin duster she had on that, despite the heat, he'd caught the house-proud little gal hard at housekeeping. The duster she wore was over-sized and shapeless, but he could still see more of her shape than she might have wanted him to, thanks to the way the thin poplin clung to damp bare skin.

She looked surprised if not dismayed to see him. She waved him in with her feather duster, saying, "Come in. I hope you don't have news too grim about my poor brother. You wouldn't be back this soon if you hadn't caught him, I know. But please tell me you took him *alive*, at least."

He removed his Stetson and waited until she'd led him into her parlor and seated him on her sofa before he told her, "I never caught up with him, dead or alive. That's likely because he was never in any of the places I was led to look for him. I don't like to boast. But it has been my experience that when I can't cut a fugitive's trail he just can't be out ahead of me. So I come back to where the trail *started* to start looking better. I may as well begin by informing you, formally, that the federal search warrant made out by the Denver District Court to them army men is still in force until such time as your brother is found on or about these premises."

She laughed weakly. "Good heavens, I told them and all the other lawmen who've tramped through this house that they were welcome to poke about all they liked, with or *without* a warrant. But before you begin, I'd better serve you some coffee and cake. For you'll surely be here some time if you expect to find Joseph in this house at this late date!"

He thanked her for the offer but said it was too hot for such a notion. She rose anyway and said, "Speak for yourself. If you don't need some coffee to clear your head right now, *I* do. This heat must be getting to my poor head. I don't understand one thing you've said so far."

She moved back to her kitchen, leaving him to stare at the four walls a spell. He was dying for a smoke, but he saw no ashtrays in sight and he doubted she shared his scientific theory that tobacco ash was hard on carpet beetles.

He could see she'd laundered her lace curtains and gone over the wallpaper with a sponge since his last visit. But there were still cleaner patches, mostly oval in design, where less tidy stuff had once hung on the walls. He was still thinking about that when she came back in with a silver service on a silver tray and put it down on the small teak table near the sofa.

As she took her own seat in the plush chair across from him he saw she'd filled two cups despite his disinclination. She asked if he preferred cream or sugar and he said neither. So she picked up her own cup and leaned back, toying with the buttons of her duster with her free hand as she smiled and said, "I like mine strong

173

and black, too. Now, what was it you were saying about my poor little brother?"

"I don't want nobody accusing me of tricking 'em later. So I'd best tell you, now, that on my way from the Union Depot to my office in the federal building I saw fit to stop at the county hall of records and the main post office just a few doors away. I have found that, even when folk don't leave a trail on the hard soil of summer, you can often get a line on them by following the paper trail we all leave filed here and there."

She was working on another button, lower down, as she said, "I hope my brother's school records and such verified everything I told you about him."

Longarm nodded and said, "He was more pathetic than even you or your neighbors may have been willing to tell a stranger. He was so lackluster in school that a kindly teacher had his head examined. The doctor's report was in with his poor report cards and such. It says he seemed to be stunted in growth, with poor hand and eye coordination. His brain just made it to what they writ down as dull-normal."

She nodded and opened another button as she said, "Everyone knew he was touched in the head, poor thing."

Longarm shook his own head. "That ain't what the doc put down. He put your brother down as a slow learner without much ambition or *imagination*. He never put down a thing about the kid being loco. How come you want to show me your tits again, ma'am? We established the last time you did it that you're a gal, and not a lunatic boy pretending to be his own sister."

She hastily regathered the front of her duster as she protested, "I wasn't trying to prove anything but how hot and stuffy it is in here right now. That other time was to show you the bruise Joseph gave me when he beat me."

Longarm nodded. "I'll take your word on the fight

you must have had with him, ma'am. You were both about the same size and weight, so it was likely an even match. But we're getting way ahead of the story. I'd best start from the beginning, now that I've been pawing through old city and county records, instead of chasing shadows along a trail that ain't been used enough to matter for years."

She leaned forward to pour more coffee in her own cup as she warned him his was getting cold. He ignored that to tell her, "In the beginning, there was a Pappa Slade, a Mamma Slade, and two little Slades, a boy and a girl, living between here and Evans Grammar School. The boy, like I just said, was puny and dim of wit and ambition. His older sister was smarter and a lot more energetic, even if her main ambition was to one day have her very own house to keep, sort of compulsed and overly tidy."

She sniffed and said, "All right, if you must know, my mother was a dear, but a lazy and careless housekeeper. You didn't have to snoop about to find *that* out. Everyone knew it."

"This is going to take all day if you keep butting in like that, ma'am. It don't take a head doctor to savvy that all-too-familiar pattern. Slovenly housekeepers raise compulsed neat daughters, and vice versa. You wanted your own house to keep, a lot neater. So you married Tom Banes, young, so's you could be the mistress of your own home, and tidy it up all you wanted."

"Is that a crime?" she asked disdainfully.

"I ain't got to criminal charges yet. Since it's your house, I can't even say it was wrong for you to cart all your late husband's hunting trophies back to his workshop as soon as you was rid of him."

She followed his glance to a spot above the fireplace where a moose head might have once hung and replied defensively, "I see no reason to deny that. I never shared Tom's interest in hunting and, to me, all those glassy-eyed dust-catchers were just an extra bother. As for my having gotten *rid* of anyone, I'd best point out my husband died at work, not here, of a heart seizure."

"That's true, right after he'd enjoyed the lunch you packed for him, if the time of death on record is correct. But that's a local matter, and we're getting ahead of my federal case some more. Before your husband died, your parents did. I'll accept that as natural. They was both elderly and in poor health, when you married hasty to get away from them."

"How can you be so cruel?" she protested.

He shrugged. "Sometimes it goes with this job. Cruel or not, facts is facts. So the fact is that by the time you found out you'd married a good-natured, natural slob, you also found you was *dependent* on him. As a manager at Denver Dry Goods, he made enough to support you decent enough and, by the way, the post office says all them Wild West magazines they delivered to this address was delivered in your *husband's* name, not your kid brother's."

"I could have told you that, had you asked. It never crossed my mind at the time."

He sighed and said, "I should have checked that earlier. It occured to me at the time that, for an unwelcome guest with no visible means of support, your kid brother had a lot of reading material stacked in his room. You likely hauled them out back when you tidied up after your late husband, right?"

She shook her head a bit wildly and said, "No. I *told* you Tom was interested in outdoor western notions. But he didn't save a magazine once he'd read it. He passed it on to Joseph, and Joseph never threw anything away."

Longarm raised an eyebrow. "You told me your husband tried to interest your brother in going hunting and such with him on the weekends, but that the kid preferred to mope about the house and get in the way of your dusting."

She shrugged. "What of it? That was why Tom asked him to leave, in the end. Tom said there had to be something wrong with a slugabed who'd rather *read* about cowboys than *ride* like one when he had the chance."

"Let's not worry about whether it was an easy-going brother-in-law or a vexed big sister who threw the kid out. The point is that someone did. So he was off in the army, no doubt vexing *them* with his useless ways, when your late father died, leaving *both* his kids well provided for with that trust fund at the Drover's Savings and Loan."

The young widow flashed her eyes at him as she snapped, "What of it? What a woman might or might not own in her own name is her own business, isn't it?"

"Yes, ma'am. There was nothing dislawful about your no-doubt fond father leaving you that house of theirs you still own, boarded up, a quarter-mile away."

"Are you suggesting Joseph could be hiding *there?*" she asked.

"Nope. The Denver copper badges already looked. That's how come I knew it was boarded up. County records don't show that. I agree it's smart of you to hold off putting it up for sale with real estate prices in Denver still rising, since the beef market got better, just recent."

He leaned back and caught himself reaching for a smoke without thinking. He put the thought aside and said, "The point is not that you are today a woman of independent means. The point is how you got that way. You came into modest wealth by birthright only *after* you'd stuck yourself with a husband who hung animal heads all over your walls and doubtless had other habits a fussy housewife couldn't abide. So, once you no longer needed him to support you, he—Let's say he just died young and unexpected. I got enough on my plate as it is."

She gasped and called him a son of a bitch. He chuckled and replied, "Takes one to know her own litter, I reckon. Anyway, just about the time you had this house prissed up more to your liking, your kid brother showed up on your doorstep. Slow-witted as he might have been, he'd have heard about the death of his own old man. So he offered to move back in with you and help you spend the family fortune."

She nodded and said, "That's true. I'll admit I told him he wasn't welcome and you saw the bruise he left on me. I *gave* him some money, damn it, but he wouldn't *leave*."

Longarm said, "He couldn't. He was dead. Had you waited until the army gents showed up, they'd have been glad to take him off your hands for you. But you didn't know that. You figured you was stuck with a bad penny you couldn't get rid of no other way. You killed your pesky little brother long before the army showed up to reclaim him. Then, when they showed up with that search warrant, you had to kill *them*, as well."

She stared at him owl-eyed and protested, "You must be as crazy as poor Joseph! How could you accuse a poor helpless woman of engaging in a gunfight with two experienced law officers?"

He smiled thinly and said, "That struck me as mysterious even when I considered a weakling who couldn't even aim a ball. The only way a green gunhand can drill anyone direct through the heart calls for firing point-blank at a stationary target. So you set 'em down here in this very parlor, served them refreshments as they was asking you about your fool kid brother, and, once they was dead, you just lined them up neat, as usual, over there on the floor, and—"

"Is *that* why you haven't touched your coffee?" she cut in, pointing at his cup. She laughed incredulously. "Did you really think I was trying to *poison* you?"

He nodded soberly. "Yes, ma'am. We'll no doubt find out which of them chemicals from your late husband's workshop you prefers to kill folk with, once we dig up all the bodies. It may be enough just to go by the results of your brother's autopsy, once we dig him up from under the loose paving of your carriage house. I noticed the *last* time I poked about out there that it tended to make you jumpy. Is that why you pegged them shots at me, up the hill, right after I'd left here? No offense, but Black Jack Junior wasn't a good shot at any distance."

Her head was wagging back and forth like that of a wind-up doll as she insisted, "This is incredible. First you accuse me of being some sort of Lucrezia Borgia, and then you accuse me of thinking I'm Black Jack Slade?"

"*Nobody* never thought they was Black Jack Slade. The notion your poor dumb brother *might* came to you after you'd put the bricks back over him. You wanted everyone to think he'd run off again. You knew you'd never get away with pretending to be him, in his well-fit army uniform. So you made a point of wandering about after dark in your *husband's,* not your *brother's* cowboy outfit. The hat was too big, but it served to hide your long hair when you pinned it up inside it. The chaps was too big, but just flopped wild once you'd cut 'em down to size. The man-sized shirt and gun rig served to further hide your handsome, curvy figure. You'd already established the poor puny loner was acting mighty odd by the time them army men rid in and you had to get rid of *them,* too. So that night you killed a mess of birds indeed with that one crazy act. You killed them silent and private. You had plenty of time to lead their horses over to the carriage house behind that *other* house you own."

She scowled and snapped, "What are you talking about? There were no horses out front, damn it."

He said, "There you go, butting in again. I know there was no horses here when I *arrived.* I wondered some about that, since both bodies was dressed for riding. But I let that go until later, after I'd had time to wonder how a lunatic with no visible means of support seemed to be getting around so good on mounts branded by the remount service. Getting back to how you *started* confusing hell out of me, you left things neat and tidy here, put on your wild outfit, and tore over to the Parthenon to pick that fight with me. In all modesty, I'm well known in downtown Denver, so you wasn't taking the chance you wanted it to *look* like when I thought a mean little cuss with a family resemblance to a more civilized sister started up with me. You'd learned the words if not the right tune to that dumb song about Black Jack Slade from the pile of pulp paper that had inspired your act in the first place. I reckon you kept a more full account of that old, dead gunslick's misdeeds for further research. That was why the pile had yarns about just about everyone, real or made up, *but* the real Black Jack, right?"

She smiled triumphantly. "I knew you had to be suffering heatstroke! Your insane accusations fall completely apart as soon as I point out I was with *you,* in your own quarters, the night my crazy brother shot up that canteen in far-off Fort Halleck!"

He told her, "No, they don't. The railroad gives away timetables free for the asking. We both know Julesburg is less than four hours away by rail. You didn't have to account for your time riding up there in broad day. The army men staked out here were more interested in the possible movements of your kid brother, not where *you* might or might not be at a given moment. So after you got off at Julesburg, mayhaps wearing that same shapeless summer duster over a wilder outfit, you checked into the hotel as a secretary gal stuck between trains. Then you hired that pony cart to go for a late-afternoon spin out across the lone prairie. Once you found it lone enough, at sunset, you took off the duster, put on that big hat, and crept onto the unguarded post as Black Jack Slade. All you had to do after the wild

180

shoot-up was beat the news back to town in that pony cart, looking less wild, and wait for the next train back to Denver. Nobody notices mousy-looking *gals* at times of such confusion."

"I was with *you,* damn it!" she insisted.

He nodded, but said, "Later that night. Just as you'd planned. You offered to go with me, after yourself, and hinted at an even better offer, no doubt hoping I'd know better than to take you up on either. Once news of the trouble in Julesburg reached us, you had more freedom of action, because both me and them army men lit out after a dead man we thought was pretending to be another dead man."

He paused to shake his head at her sadly before he went on, "You should have ended it there, Miss Flora. You'd already hurt lots of innocent gents who'd never done you wrong. But you was feeling too pleased with yourself to quit while you were ahead. Knowing the original Black Jack had haunted the old Overland Trail, you wanted to lead me further astray along the same. So, once again playing your innocent female self, you took them dead army men's mounts with you, by rail this time. You got off mayhaps half a day's ride from Scott's Bluff. The county seat at Gering works best, since it's on another rail line."

"I defy you to produce a stock freight ticket in my name!" she cut in, wild-eyed.

He said, "That's silly, ma'am. Nobody with a lick of sense would board a combo under her own name if she was *half* as slick as you. You could have told 'em you was the Queen of Rumania and they wouldn't have cared, as long as you paid cash for transporting yourself and two nondescript bay horses. After you detrained with 'em, wherever, you rode over to and through Scott's Bluff as yourself, sizing it up. Then, after dark, you left the one mount tethered just outside town, rode back in as Black Jack Junior, and gunned that poor blacksmith for no other reason than to convince us your kid brother was alive, if not exactly well. You shot that last victim in the head after I'd told you, and *you alone,* that a heart-shot gent sometimes had a whiff of fight left in him. Couldn't you have settled for just scaring him, the way you scared everyone else up there?"

She insisted she didn't know what on earth he was talking about. "Sure you do. You rode out aboard that buckskin, got rid of such a well-known mount, and rode back the way you'd come, as a shapeless mousy little gal aboard a bay nobody was looking for. The excitement must have been enough for even *you* by then. One mount running off on you so unexpected and all them drunks yelling at you must have left you with the feeling there could be more risk to the game than you'd bargained for. So *that* was when you quit.

"It was easy. You just had to bury Black Jack Junior somewhere on the prairie, turn the horse loose far east of where we was hunting you to the west, and if it's been picked up by anyone at all, they might or might not run the brand and keep it for their own. All you had to do, then, was get back to this house you seem so fond of, and dust it all you wanted to, as I hunted for nobody much in all the wrong places. Had I not got stuck in one place long enough to start hunting with my brain instead of my restless nature, I'd no doubt be pestering folk in Salt Lake or Virginia City about now. But, with the help of a friend who asked why *both* Black Jacks couldn't be dead and buried, I got inspired, and here I am, like another bad penny."

She was staring at him like she felt sorry for him as she said, "Heavens, what an imagination you must have! It's all too easy to prove how innocent even my *coffee* is!"

Before he could stop her, she had picked up his cup and drained it at one gulp.

He leaped up, ran into her kitchen, and poured milk

from her icebox and mustard powder from her cupboard into a handy mixing bowl. But by the time he could get back to her she'd already taken the table and silver service to the floor with her, and was writhing like an earthworm caught by sunrise on a slate walk, glaring up at him with a frozen snarl that might have scared the real Black Jack out of a saloon.

He dropped to one knee on the coffee-soaked rug and tried to force some of the hasty emetic between her clenched teeth. But he only managed to spill it down her jaw. Then her heels stopped drumming and her stiff spine went limp. He put the mixing bowl aside and felt for a pulse. He lowered her head to the rug and rose to stare morosely down as he told the pathetic sight at his feet, "Any lawyer worth his salt would have got you off on an insanity plea. I reckon it's just as well you tried to the end to keep things *tidy.* You just stay put, and I'll go get the undertaker for you."

He put on his hat and left her there, closing her front door neatly after him as he stepped out. As he strode off along the sun-baked walk, two little old ladies were coming up it, under their sunbonnets and parasols. One recognized him from having seen him about the neighborhood before. She smiled at him sweetly and asked, "And how are you this afternoon, young man? Do you think we're due for a break in this awful heat wave?"

He ticked his hatbrim to them both as he answered, "No, ma'am. But, to tell the truth, I don't mind feeling warm, when I consider all the alternatives."

Watch for

LONGARM AND THE BIG POSSE

one hundred and fifth novel in the bold
LONGARM series from Jove

coming in September!

LONGARM

Explore the exciting Old West with one of the men who made it wild!

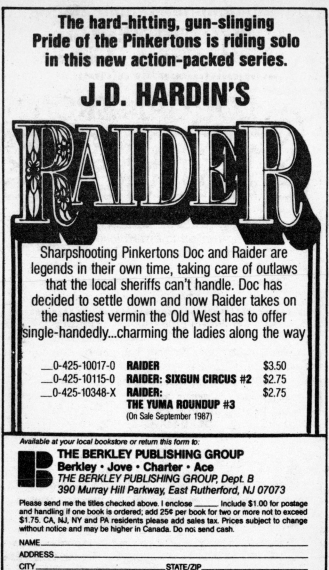